Dear Reader,

The book you've just bought from my "Second Chances" series is truly evidence of the second chances God gives us. The books in this series have been published before, some by Dell, some by Harlequin, others by Silhouette and HarperCollins. I was a Christian when I entered the romance market in 1983, hoping to take the world by storm. What I found, instead, was that the world took *me* by storm. One compromise led to another, until my books did not read like books written by a Christian. Not only were they not pleasing to God, but they embraced a worldview that opposed Christ's teachings. In the interest of being successful, I had compartmentalized my faith. I trusted Christ for my salvation, but not much else. Like the Prodigal Son, I had taken my inheritance and left home to do things my own way.

I love that parable because it so reflects my life. My favorite part is when Jesus said, "But while he was still a long way off, his father saw him . . ." I can picture that father scanning the horizon every day, hoping for his son's return. God did that for me. While I was still a long way off, God saw me coming. Early in 1994, when I yearned to be closer to God and realized that my writing was a wall between us, that my way had not been the best way, I promised God that I would never write anything again that did not glorify him. At that moment, it was as if God came running out to meet me. I gave up my secular career and began to write Christian books.

Shortly after I signed a contract for Zondervan to publish my suspense series, "The Sun Coast Chronicles," something extraordinary happened. The rights to some of my earlier romance novels were given back to me, and I was free to do whatever I wanted with them. At first, I thought of shelving them, but then, in God's gentle way, he reminded me that I was free to rewrite them, and this time, get them right. So I set about to rewrite these stories the way God originally intended them.

As you read these stories, keep in mind that they're not just *about* second chances, they *are* second chances. I hope you enjoy them.

In Christ,
Terri Blackstock

Second Chances

NEVER AGAIN GOOD-BYE

TERRI BLACKSTOCK

ZondervanPublishingHouse

Grand Rapids, Michigan

A Division of HarperCollinsPublishers

Never Again Good-bye
Copyright © 1996 by Terri Blackstock

Requests for information should be addressed to:

ZondervanPublishingHouse
Grand Rapids, Michigan 49530

Library of Congress Cataloging-in-Publication Data

Blackstock, Terri, 1957–
    Never again good-bye / Terri Blackstock.
       p.   cm. — (Second chances)
    ISBN: 0-310-20707-X (pbk.)
     I. Title.   II. Series: Blackstock, Terri, 1957–   Second chances.
PS3552.L34285N48   1996
813'.54—dc20   96–17275
                                               CIP

Published in association with the literary agency of Alive Communications, Inc., 1465 Kelly Johnson Blvd.,Suite 320, Colorado Springs, CO 80920

Interior design by Sue Vandenberg Koppenol
Edited by Dave Lambert and Lori Walburg

Printed in the United States of America

97 98 99 00 01 02 / ❖ DC/ 10 9 8 7 6 5 4

This book is lovingly dedicated to the Nazarene,
with amazement for all the second chances he's given me.

Acknowledgments

I'd like to thank my friends from both sides of adoption, who shared their painful stories with me for the sake of this book. Special thanks to my daughters, Michelle and Marie, through whom I've known all the joys and wonders of motherhood.

CHAPTER ONE

Kidnappers don't look like criminals, Wes Grayson thought as he moved closer behind the young woman he'd been watching for the last half hour. At least, that was what he'd told his daughter so many times. They looked trustworthy and pleasant, and that was how they deceived.

Why, then, was it so hard for him to believe that this five-foot-three, hundred-pound woman, who looked barely old enough to qualify as a legal adult, was about to strike?

Yet he'd seen her behavior himself, and it was suspicious, if not threatening. Moving closer without making a sound, he held his hands poised to catch her if she tried to run when she realized she'd been seen. The shutter of her camera clicked, and she stepped deeper into the shade of the pine trees that edged the park, adjusted her lens, and focused again.

With eyes narrowed in a natural squint from years of construction work in the harsh Louisiana sun, Wes followed her aim to the children scaling the monkey bars and watched the camera pan to the right as his seven-year-old daughter left the cluster of her friends and went to her baby-sitter. A vein in his temple throbbed with the pressure of waiting. Why had the police department taken so long to respond to his call? Did they think she'd hang around indefinitely?

As if in reaction to his thoughts, a Shreveport PD squad car pulled up and two uniformed officers got out, hiking up the waists of their pants and glancing around as if wondering which tree to settle under for their afternoon nap. The woman spotted them and snapped her camera back in its case. As she took a step back, Wes moved within grasping distance.

She smelled of apricots, he thought as the early spring breeze rustled the black wisps of hair that had escaped from her long braid. Criminals didn't smell like apricots, did they? And they didn't have that look of vulnerable fragility or wear designer jeans and silk blouses. But this one did. Drawing his brows together, he watched her partial profile as she looked across the park at his daughter.

Her suspicious interest in Amy sent a chill of panic through him, and Wes clenched his teeth, silently willing the policemen to hurry. But when they stopped at his baby-sitter, who had no idea that he had been standing in the shadows behind a potential kidnapper for the last half hour, Wes had no choice but to take matters into his own hands.

Carefully he reached out and grabbed her arm.

She jumped and tried to jerk free. "Let me go!"

"Why?" he asked through his teeth. "So you can keep stalking innocent children?"

The depth of her dark eyes as they searched his was unexpected, and for a fleeting second, he wondered if a criminal would really look so scared. Wouldn't there be some harshness in her eyes, some cold glint of evil intent that couldn't be concealed?

"Stalking?" she asked quickly. "Is that what you think?"

"You tell me," he said, remembering the woman who had wept when her child was kidnapped from a park across town the previous week. He and other members of his church had joined the effort to search for her, but to no avail. "I want some answers, and they'd better be good."

"Answers to what? I haven't done anything."

He smiled at the guilt in her voice, guilt that told him he was not making a mistake. "Tell it to the cops," he said.

"The cops?" Her voice was high and incredulous, and the woman swung around, this time managing to free her arm. "You called the police?" A look of terror sprang to her eyes, and her lips trembled. "Why? What did I do?"

She was backing away, trying, Wes realized, to gain enough distance to break into a run. Before she could get far he grabbed her again and, in one swift movement, twisted her arm behind her back, immobilizing her completely.

"Let go of me!" she hissed again. "And tell me what I've done!"

His voice was equally harsh. "You've been sneaking around here snapping pictures of my daughter."

"Your—your daughter?" Her voice caught, and her gaze snapped to the child on the playground. "She's your daughter?"

Her question was as close to an admission of guilt as he needed. His lips grew taut against gritted teeth, and he jerked her arm harder, heard her gasp, and told himself that he was right: She *was* after his daughter. Amy had almost been the next child to go. Roughly he pulled her out of the shadows and toward the growing crowd of people at the center of the park.

"Wait!" Despite the grueling twist of her arm and the pain it inflicted, the woman held back. "I don't want to go over there."

"Well, that's just too bad, isn't it?"

But she ground in her heels and refused to move without being dragged. "Please," she bit out. "Make the policemen come over here. I don't want to frighten the children."

Wes stopped at her words and studied her curiously. What did she care about frightening the children? Was she afraid of blowing her cover, ruining her chances of earning their trust so she could take them of their own free will? Or was it real concern? Did she care about their ability to sleep easily at night, about tainting the joy they found in the park?

Still holding her against him, Wes glanced toward his daughter and considered the woman's request. She was right. The children would be told. Things didn't need to be confused by creating an uproar. He saw his baby-sitter stand up, spot him, and point him out. The policemen started toward them.

"I haven't done anything," the woman muttered, looking over her shoulder with eyes that could have convinced him of her innocence if he hadn't witnessed her actions himself. She seemed more afraid than he was. "They can't arrest me for taking pictures."

"They can if they connect you with the kidnapping in town last week."

He felt her shiver under his grip.

"It's not what you think," she choked. "I'm not a kidnapper! I'm a photographer. I'm working on a photo layout about Louisiana youth."

"Save it," he said. "Photographers don't sneak around and hide in shadows to get their pictures. And they don't single out one child and use three rolls of film on her."

Sending a beseeching look toward the sky, she gave up the argument, lifting her chin defiantly as the policemen approached. Compressing her quivering lips and hardening her eyes, she listened as Wes related his suspicions.

"Have any identification?" one officer asked in a long southern drawl.

"Identification?" she asked. Her eyes flashed nervously to Wes's, and her throat convulsed. "Yes . . . I have it here." Wes let her go, and her hands trembled as they dug into her camera case. She pulled out her driver's license, studied it a moment with worried eyes, then handed it to the officer.

"Elaine Fields," the officer read aloud.

Wes felt her eyes assessing him with a fear that went deeper than the obvious. She seemed to be anticipating trouble, almost as if she expected him to recognize her name.

"Laney," she said, her eyes still on him. "They call me Laney."

When he didn't respond through word or expression, her shoulders seemed to relax. Did he know her? he wondered. Was he supposed to?

Before he could wonder further, his daughter saw him and shouted out a joyful "Daddy!"

The child bolted toward him, and Wes saw the woman close her eyes then open them again and focus on the top of a pine tree. She turned away from him as he swept the child into his arms and hushed her by whispering into her ear.

"You can't arrest me for taking pictures," the woman repeated in a barely audible voice. "I haven't broken any laws."

"No," one of the officers agreed. "But we can take you in for questioning. And Mr. Grayson, we'll need you to come along to fill out a complaint."

"What did she do, Daddy?" the girl asked in a hushed voice.

Before he could answer, the woman swung toward the police officers. "Fine. Let's get this over with. Take me in for questioning." Without waiting for a response, she started toward the police car.

Wes stood frozen for a moment, amazed at her sudden acquiescence. Why was she being so compliant? He set his daughter down and stared at the woman climbing into the backseat of the police car. The proud lift of her chin was at odds with the pain in her dark eyes. Who was Laney Fields? he wondered as he took his daughter back to the baby-sitter.

After arranging for the sitter to take Amy home, he went to his own car. Laney Fields's eyes said she was an innocent prepared for the worst, but her actions said she was a criminal preparing to *do* the worst. His mind said she was up to no good; his gut said his mind might have led him wrong again. Bracing himself for the remote possibility that he'd made a mistake, Wes went to the police station to file his complaint.

A mistake, Laney thought as she sat in the questioning room at the local precinct. She should never have been caught. He might have recognized her name, might have realized who she was. But apparently he hadn't. She realized now that he had never heard the name Laney Fields, had never known what connection it had to his life or to his daughter's. Glancing down at her fingertips, she noticed she had absentmindedly scraped a layer of skin off with her nails. She looked up at Wes Grayson, who sat across from her with his written complaint form on the table in front of him, his green eyes imprisoning her before she had even been charged with a crime. She didn't blame him at all. He had every right to suspect her of being a kidnapper. Had she been in his position, she probably would have jumped to the same conclusion. Why had she believed she could blend into the background and watch the girl from a distance without being noticed?

The silence seemed heavy, making the room insufferably hot. A fan in the corner circulated the stifling air with a low, maddening hum. The clock on the wall ticked off agonizing seconds, its slight clicks reminding her of dripping water in a torture chamber. Her father would have had a field day with this, she thought, if he had lived to see it. His disappointing, stubborn daughter detained in a police station. Whether she had broken a law or not, he would have been sure that such punishment was well deserved. And arguing with him would have been pointless, for doing so would have only made her more derelict in his eyes.

But he wasn't here, she thought. Just an uninterested, perspiring policeman, who seemed on the brink of exhaustion, and her accuser, whose probing regard made her feel unbearably trapped. She glanced across the table, noted his short clean fingernails as they drummed out a judgmental rhythm on the table, the rugged texture of fingers that had known physical labor and thrived on it, the lack of male jewelry, either rings or watch, that would have offered clues to the man. He watched her with fathomless green eyes, eyes that would have drawn her in if they hadn't been frightening her away, eyes that seemed to wonder and question and, above all, accuse.

The door opened, momentarily halting the maddening thrumming of his fingers, and the officer who had gone to check out her story came back in. "Seems she's telling the truth. She's a photographer, and *Heritage* magazine confirmed that she's working on a layout for them."

Laney tried to keep the overwhelming relief from her sigh. She would have to thank her editor the next time she spoke to him. Better yet, she thought, she'd go ahead and do that job. As yet it had been only a vague idea mentioned in passing on the phone.

Wes was not appeased, however. His finger came up to stroke his lips and his eyes narrowed. "The fact that she's a photographer doesn't mean a thing. She's obviously good with a camera. I want to know why she was taking pictures of my daughter."

Laney felt her stomach churning. It was time for explanations, time for control. Time to hold herself together and make her lie sound true. "Mr. Grayson, she's a beautiful child. I thought she represented what I was trying to capture."

"Exactly my point."

She leaned wearily back in her chair and wished that someone would open the window so she could breathe. "I mean photographically. You can't argue that she stands out in a crowd."

Not flattered, Wes turned to the policeman, raking a hand through hair the color of mahogany, streaked with blond where the sun had favored it. He wasn't going to give up easily, she realized. "How can you be sure she isn't the one who kidnapped that child last week?"

"Two good reasons," the officer said. "One is that her alibi checks out. She's been in town for only four days."

"Maybe she's working with someone else."

When the officer shook his head, Wes slammed his hands on the table. "What's the second reason then?"

The officer pulled out his chair and slumped into it, rubbing his face. "About ten minutes ago I got word that that child was found this afternoon. It was a case of parental abduction. Divorced father who wanted custody."

The scowl on Wes's face faded by degrees. "After the scare they gave us all. We turned this town upside down." Slouching back in his chair, he covered his face with rough hands and scrutinized Laney over his fingertips. Her big, haunted eyes reflected intense relief, and he realized he *had* made a mistake. A whopper. He'd been accused of being an overprotective father before, but this was ridiculous even to him.

"Then I don't suppose you have any more reason to hold me?" she asked.

The officer shrugged. "You can go now. Sorry for the inconvenience."

Laney stood up, fighting dizziness in the wake of such emotional havoc. Her hands still trembled, and her face was even paler than it had been earlier.

Neither expecting nor wanting an apology, she looked back at Wes and recognized the self-defeated glimmer in his eyes. "That's all right. I can understand the scare. Next time I'll be more careful." For a moment she kept her eyes on the man who had frightened her. The man who now knew her name and her face and would notice her the next time she went near Amy. The man who had ended her plans, shattered her hopes, and made it impossible for her to end the torment she'd suffered for seven years. *Amy's father*, she thought with a shiver. *Amy's father.*

Laney left quickly and was just outside the station when Wes Grayson caught up to her. He caught her arm to stop her, and she jerked free. "I'm getting tired of you grabbing me that way!"

He raised his hand in innocence and took a step back. "I just wanted to—"

"To what?" she asked. "To find some other unsolved crime to pin on me? This day has turned out bad enough. Can't you just leave me alone?"

Wes set his jaw. "Look, you're the one who was sneaking around in the bushes. I just followed my instincts."

"Great instincts," she retorted.

"You're not too easy to apologize to, are you?"

Laney laughed dryly. "Apologize? Was that an apology?"

"Yeah," he said, indignant.

Laney shook her head and started to her car. "You, Mr. Grayson, are a real jerk!" Her braid swayed viciously across her hips as she walked.

"What are you so hot about?" he asked, catching up to her again. "They didn't even book you."

Laney reached her car, the foreign sports car that the policeman had been so anxious to drive to the station for her, and searched through her purse for her keys. "They didn't have to book me. They humiliated me in a public park and dragged me in like some common criminal."

"I said I was sorry!"

"No, you didn't!"

They stood glaring at each other for an electric moment, searing green eyes against furious black ones. Finally, Wes straightened and thrust out his chin.

"If you can't accept an apology, it's not my fault," he mumbled, starting to his own car. Then, under his breath, he added, "And I'm not a jerk."

Laney ignored him as she got into her car and slammed the door.

Yes, he was a jerk, Wes told himself that night. A big, stupid, paranoid jerk!

He rubbed the bridge of his nose and gave a low chuckle. If he hadn't been so caught up in his Clint Eastwood routine, he would have realized he'd been strongly attracted to Laney Fields. That was why he had noticed her suspicious behavior in the first place. The first woman he'd been attracted to in a year, and what did he do? Instead of asking her out, he'd had her arrested!

He looked at his reflection in the window and raised his soup can in a toast. "Nice going, Grayson," he said with a wry grin. He chuckled, keeping his voice quiet so as not to wake Amy. "A real Casanova. A little more of that charm, and you would have had her on her knees." He shook his head. At least he could laugh about it now. He only wished *she* could. Maybe then he could start over and actually walk up to her and say, "Hi, do you come here often?" or whatever it was men said to women these days.

Of course, he could always start with an apology. Maybe he could even get her to smile if he admitted to being a jerk. It might give her a new idea for a story. "Paranoid Father Chokes on Apology" would be infinitely more interesting than the one on Louisiana youth.

What could it hurt, after all? Now that he knew she was no criminal, he could admit that he was overwhelmingly attracted to her . . . even though she was several years younger than he.

He reluctantly dragged his mind back to the apology. If nothing else, it would give him an excuse to see her again. He raised his can for another toast. "To second chances," he said with a smile. His reflection gave him a deprecating smirk. He only hoped Laney Fields had a soft spot in her heart for self-admitted jerks who learned humility very quickly.

CHAPTER TWO

Laney stood in the red haze cast by the safelight in her makeshift darkroom and watched with enchanted eyes as the child's face emerged from memory to reality in the space of a few moments. Black pigtails appeared . . . dark, wondrous eyes that beheld the beauties and mysteries of the world . . . and a missing front tooth. They were all there, all parts of the child that, until now, had seemed no more than a longing dreamed up by a lonely young woman.

They named her Amy, she thought as she set her mouth in a compressed line to keep it from trembling. Amy Grayson.

Drawing a controlled breath, she pulled out the photograph and hung it on the line above her, next to others like it. Even more littered the dining room table. She held her eyes wide to keep the tears at bay, arched her brows in pained perusal, and stepped back to study the prints again.

"She's so beautiful," she whispered, her words laced with the despair of one who sees but cannot touch.

Now she couldn't even see her. Laney couldn't watch her soccer games, couldn't attend the ballet recitals and school plays, couldn't blend in at the park, as she had planned when she'd moved back to Shreveport. They knew her now, and she would be too conspicuous. It was over. All over.

The tears found their way out, and she fled from the room. She wouldn't need the darkness anymore—she had more within her than she'd ever escape. And she had enough pictures. Enough mementos. Enough reminders that life was never fair. Laney dropped into a chair and covered her quivering mouth. It was useless to have returned to Shreveport, and yet she'd had no other choice. She was a woman driven by regret and injustice and the vivid memories that had driven her away. And she had the desperate need to know that her decisions had been for the best.

But she couldn't change the situation now, not when she saw the bright smile in the child's glimmering eyes. Despite the twists and schemes of fate, life seemed to have turned out well for Amy.

Life had been good to Laney Fields, Wes Grayson thought as he stood at the door of the Tudor-style house the next day. He wondered if he'd written down the right address. He had gotten it from the police report, but he hadn't expected more than a two-bedroom apartment. She looked too young to own an upper-middle-class home of her own . . . and certainly she couldn't afford it on the pay of a freelance photographer. When she had declined to call anyone from the police station the day before, he had assumed she wasn't married. He hoped he was right. It wasn't like him to show up unexpectedly at the home of someone he'd met under bizarre circumstances, but her phone number hadn't been listed. Giving a bewildered shrug, he pushed the doorbell and smiled at the eight-note Westminster sequence that followed. It was certainly more attractive than the old tried-and-true "ding-dong," but he wondered if it would get anyone's attention inside.

He glanced toward the three-car garage and saw her white sports car. She was probably in the back, he thought. No one stayed inside on a beautiful Saturday.

He followed the path that led to the back of the house, to the pool with its water rippling in the breeze. He saw her then on her knees pulling weeds out of a garden that was overgrown. Her knees and hands were covered with dirt, and her long black hair was tied back with a shoestring.

For a moment he stood back and quietly watched her, wondering how on earth he could have found her so threatening yesterday. She looked so small, so fragile, and he couldn't help feeling ashamed of himself. Suddenly he was nervous and wondered at the wisdom of his coming here. He thought of leaving before she noticed he was here, and took a step backward. But he didn't want to go.

So he stood there quietly for a moment, waiting for the right time to make his presence known.

The gravelly sound of a man clearing his throat startled Laney, and she jumped and swung around, her eyes widening at the sight of him. "What are you doing here? Why didn't you say something?"

"I was going to," he said quickly.

Her cheeks reddened as she got to her feet, and she wiped her dirty hands on her jeans.

"I . . . I thought I should come by and say . . . uh . . . about yesterday . . ."

She was covered with dirt and perspiration, and suddenly self-conscious, she started toward the door. "I have to change. I'll be right back."

"It's hot," he said. "Do you mind if I wait inside?"

Laney straightened and glanced through the glass door to the den. The archway leading to the dining room was open, and she'd left photos of Amy scattered on the table. But if she let him in, he'd probably just sit down and wait. He'd have no reason to wander into the dining room. And if she hurried . . .

Reluctantly, she led him in, but he didn't sit down. His standing made her nervous.

"What brings you here, Mr. Grayson?" she asked, deciding to get the conversation over with as soon as possible while trying to look as dignified as she could with filthy hands and knees. "Did you think of some new way to send me up the creek?"

"River," Wes said with a smile.

"What?"

"It's up the river. And, no, that's not what I came for." He glanced out the bay window that looked out over the pool, and his amusement gave way to a serious expression that looked more at home on his face. His thumb scratched over the T-shirt with the words "Bound for Glory" printed across the chest.

He was a Christian, then. The realization made her feel nervous, exposed, as though he stood in judgment of all the darkness in her life.

21

"I came because I owe you an apology," he said. "A real one. You were right. I was a jerk yesterday."

Laney looked down at the floor, praying that he'd sit down so she could go change. *Just accept his apology and he'll leave*, she told herself. "We were both under a lot of stress in a very unusual set of circumstances."

"Yeah, but I could have handled it a lot better."

"Possibly," she agreed. "But it's over now. It's not good to dwell on things. Just sit down and—"

"I hoped you'd let me make it up to you," he cut in. His eyes moved back to hers, and their intensity startled her.

"Please, Mr. Grayson—"

"Wes. Call me Wes. I mean . . . I'm not *that* much older than you. How old are you, anyway?"

She sighed with frustration. "I'm twenty-five."

"See?" he asked with a weak smile. "I'm only eight years older. Not old enough to call Mister."

"Whatever." Unable to use his first name, she struggled back to her original thought. "You don't owe me anything."

"You mean you don't care that I won't be able to sleep until I redeem myself?"

"Not in the least."

His smile came easily this time. "Come on; I just want to clear my conscience."

Crossing her dirty arms, she sighed. "How did you want to redeem yourself? Paint the house; clean out the pool?"

His grin broadened, and he rubbed his chin. "I had something less physical in mind."

"Like what?"

"Like maybe buying you lunch."

"A hamburger for a criminal record?" She gave an exaggerated shrug. "Sounds fair."

"Ah, come on," he said on a laugh. "That won't go on your record. And I was thinking more along the lines of pizza. Amy's at a birthday party, so I have some free time today."

Laney's face darkened at the child's name, and sadness found its way into her black eyes again. Her head moved slowly from side to side. "I can't go for pizza with you."

"Why not?"

"Because."

He nodded to her hallway and planted his feet firmly, as if he had no intention of settling for that answer. "Go ahead and change clothes. We can talk about it when you're more comfortable."

She studied him for a moment, like a wide-eyed doe preparing to dart away. Would he stay there, or was he the kind to walk around while he waited? Could she change fast enough to be back before he lost interest in the view of the backyard? "All right," she said finally, realizing she had to chance it. "I'll just be a minute." She dashed down the hall and into her bedroom.

"Nice house," Wes called to her after she left. She heard the couch squeak as he got up, his footsteps as he ambled across the room. Was he looking at the family pictures on her wall? She tried to move faster. "Do you live here alone?" he called.

Laney searched her closet, pulled out a pair of jeans and a white pullover shirt. "It was my father's," she called back breathlessly. "He died a year ago. I just decided to move back."

"So you're from here originally?"

Laney pulled the jeans on. It was good to keep him talking. Maybe he'd stay in the den. "Yes. I've been living in Houston for the past several years. I left home when I was pretty young."

"Did you go to college in Houston?"

"Yes," she said.

"So did you—" His question was cut off abruptly.

"What?" she asked. There was no answer, and the silence seemed more eloquent than a million words. Suddenly she knew what had silenced him, what had stunned him. Her heart stopped, and she grabbed hold of her dresser. Holding her breath, she listened in frozen terror then forced herself to move. Her voice cracked, "Mr. Grayson?"

No answer.

Bracing herself, Laney walked out of the bedroom, looked across the den, and saw that he stood in the archway of the dining room. His back was rigid as he glared at hundreds of photos of his daughter, pictures she had taken over the last three days.

Dizzying fear coursed through her as he turned to confront her, and the murderous anger in his eyes made her back away.

"You have five seconds to tell me who you are and what in the name of heaven you're up to."

"I told you," she said on a thin rush of breath. "I'm working on a—"

"I'm warning you," he hissed, his eyes assaulting her. His anger was a tangible thing, hardening his face. "Don't give me that Louisiana youth stuff again because I don't buy it. You've been following Amy." His hand trembling with rage, he snatched up two of the snapshots. "She wore that dress three days ago. And this one . . . she had that on the other night. Have you just been stalking her everywhere, waiting to grab her when you had the chance?"

"No!" she said, daring to reach for the pictures he held.

He jerked them away, and she flinched, expecting him to strike her on the downswing.

When his coiled hand only dropped to his side, she said, "I didn't mean any harm. I just . . ." Her words trailed off. He wouldn't accept another lie, Laney realized, and she could not tell him the truth. Bracing herself for his justifiable attack, she dropped her head in defeat.

"What do you have to gain?" he asked in a quiet voice that was infinitely more intimidating than a full-fledged yell. "I have a small, struggling construction company that I may not be able to keep above water much longer. Even if I sold everything I own, I still couldn't come up with much ransom."

Laney was outraged. "I don't want your money!"

"Then why? Is stalking helpless children just a sickness?"

"Stop using that word! I wasn't stalking her. I wasn't even going to touch her," she said, despair quivering in her voice. "I just wanted pictures. Something of her that I could keep. Is that so wrong?"

"Yes, it's wrong!" he cried, the words lashing across her. "You should be locked up." He slammed a fist into her wall, startling her, and she felt the impact of it vibrate through to her soul. "Why Amy? Why not one of those other children?"

Tears burned Laney's eyes, spilled down her cheeks, and her trembling hand rose to cover her mouth.

"Answer me! I want to know before I have you taken away!"

She took a step back and found herself against the wall. Wes moved dangerously closer and grabbed Laney's chin, forcing her to meet his eyes. "Answer me!"

She closed her eyes tightly, fighting the words that waited to be spoken. Tears escaped, and her knees threatened to fold beneath her.

"Answer me!" he rasped, his breath hot against her face, snapping her last tenets of control.

"Because she's my daughter!" she blurted. "She's my little girl."

CHAPTER THREE

Wes's rage vanished as an expression of complete shock leached the blood from his face. He dropped his hand and stumbled back, then ran a shaky hand through his tousled hair. "You," he whispered after a moment. "You were her mother?"

Laney wiped her tears and turned away, pressing her face against the wall. Her voice was a high-pitched, broken stream of words. "The birth certificate . . . and the adoption papers . . . are on the table with the pictures. They're proof."

She heard him shuffling papers behind her, his uneven breath that of a man whose worst fears had been realized. He groaned when he saw the proof. "How? How did you get these? The file was supposed to be sealed."

"I have money." Her voice steadied to a lifeless monotone. "I used it."

The seconds ticked by, and she felt him reviewing the signs that told him she was no imposter. "I should have seen it," he whispered brokenly. "She looks like you. Black hair, dark eyes, small frame, the trace of Indian heritage . . ." He turned away and expelled a jagged sigh. "You can't have her back. She's mine."

The words ripped through her. She swung around, and her voice was barely audible with the force of its soft anguish. "Don't you think I know that?" she sobbed. "I gave up my rights to her seven years ago, whether I wanted to or not. She's a happy child. I'd rather die than spoil that."

He studied her for a moment, gauging her eyes for something he could trust, something he could believe in, then dropped his focus to his tennis shoe. "How do I know I can believe you? You've lied to me about everything so far."

"I'm not lying about this. What more have I got to lose?"

What more have I got to lose? Heaven help me, Wes thought. Amy was all he had left. Absolutely all. He focused his misting eyes on the ceiling and bit his lip until he drove out the color. "I want you to stay away from her. You've got your precious pictures, but I don't want you anywhere near her again."

"Don't worry," Laney said ruefully. "She thinks I'm a criminal now, remember? She saw the police taking me away yesterday."

"Just the same, I want you to stay away from her." He clenched his hand and pressed it against his mouth. A vein in his neck throbbed, and the muscles in his temples tightened. "If it wasn't to take Amy, then why did you come back here?"

Her shaking hand went up to dry her eyes in vain, and she walked across the room to drop onto the sofa. "Because it's my home. I grew up here."

"What about your work?"

"I quit my job in Houston. I worked in the advertising department of a department store, and I do freelance photography on the side."

"So you came back here without a job, just because it's where you grew up? Why now, after seven years?"

Laney dried her face with both hands and met his piercing gaze. How could she tell him that her father's death had triggered her need to right things, that until he died she had been emotionally dead and dictated over, even though she hadn't seen him in years. "As long as I leave Amy alone, Mr. Grayson, it's none of your business why I came back here. The fact is that I'm staying."

Wes took a few steps closer and leaned over her, the pulse in his neck throbbing visibly. "I don't like it. I want you out of this town. I have enough problems without worrying what you'll do next."

"Take my word for it," she choked. "You'll probably never even see me again."

"Take your word for it," he repeated with disgust. "Under the circumstances, that's a little easier said than done."

"Try," she said. "I'd never hurt my daughter by trying to take her from the only family she knows."

Wes shifted and began to pace the floor, studied her at each turn, then slowed to a stop. "It looks like I don't have a choice. I can't force you to leave or to sign in blood that you'll make no claim on her, can I? You've backed me into a corner, and I have to trust you."

"That's right," she said quietly. "You have to trust me."

He rubbed a hand over his chin, and she noted the brown stubble that looked surprisingly dark against a complexion growing pastier by the moment.

"I hope you're a decent person," he said on a ragged sigh.

"I am," she said, lifting her chin with an unmistakable degree of pride. "It took me a long time to believe that, but I am."

Their eyes locked for a moment, and she knew he wanted desperately to believe her, to leave her house and not look back. He had to trust blindly, the way she had had to do when she left Shreveport seven years before, praying the adoptive parents were decent people. Wes swallowed with great effort, as though all his anger and fears were trapped at the back of his throat. Finally he nodded his head and started toward the double oak doors.

"Mr. Grayson?"

He stopped, leaned against the door, then reluctantly turned back to her.

Laney struggled with the question, but finally it stumbled out. "Does Amy know she's adopted?"

"Yes."

"Oh." She looked down at her hands for a moment. Bringing her misty eyes back to his, she shrugged. "She's so beautiful and so well-adjusted. Happy." Her throat filled, raising her pitch, but the words had to be said. "You and your wife are doing a wonderful job with her. I'm very grateful for that. Would you . . . would you thank her for me?"

Wes Grayson's own eyes glossed over, glimmering with a deep sadness Laney didn't understand until he spoke. "My wife's been dead for a year," he said. Then he opened the door and was gone.

Laney lay in bed that night staring into the darkness, fresh misery weighing on her heart for all the tragedies she had encountered in her life. Her mother's death came back to her, and the nights she lay in this bed awake for months afterward, groping for some reason that she deserved such severe punishment. She remembered the years that followed when her father's inability to love her had kept him distant, and the way she had tried so hard to please him in everything she'd done. But he had been a hard man, and during those years she had succeeded at nothing except failing him.

She wondered if it was that way for Amy—if she lay in bed at night weeping for her mother until she fell asleep. She wondered if Wes Grayson was the type of man who could be both mother and father to a little girl, or if Amy, too, would never quite measure up to all the things he demanded in return for having to raise her alone. She tried to put herself in Amy's shoes, and tears sprang to her eyes again. Did the little girl—who knew one mother had given her up and that a second had been taken from her—have any faith in relationships at all? Was she able to trust love, or would she grow up wary of attachments, just as Laney was? Did Wes Grayson have that wisdom in his heart that could heal the child and allow her to accept something that could never be explained? Or would she, like Laney, hand herself over, heart, body, and soul to the first boy she met who offered her the slightest hint of affection?

She got out of bed and went back to the dining room to the photographs still scattered on the table, and as it often did, her mind strayed to the boy she had been in love with over seven years ago until he had offered her money for an abortion then abandoned her when she refused.

She closed her eyes, trying to shut out the image that reeled inevitably through her mind: the coldness in her father's eyes as her body had changed from month to month; his quiet determination to take the matter out of her hands the moment the baby was born; the horror of the empty hospital cradle where her baby was supposed to be. She had never gotten over the helpless feeling of her father's betrayal and the finality of her loss.

It was her punishment, she admitted, wiping her eyes and looking down at the pictures again. She had bought into the lie that free love had no price and that one night wouldn't make a difference. She had believed that it was her body, her life, her future, and that the choice the two of them had made that night wouldn't harm anyone. Now there was a child across town who had lost two mothers.

Abandoning the pictures, Laney went back to her bedroom. The dusty pink shades of dawn invaded her room, lifting the dark and bringing with it a longing to set things right. She had promised Wes that she wouldn't make a claim on the child, and she had meant it. But that was before she'd known that Amy was being raised by a single father. That changed everything.

She lay down on her side, staring at the phone beside her bed. More tears of confusion and turmoil rolled out of her eyes. She wanted her baby back, she thought. She wanted to hold her and help to heal her grieving little heart. She wanted more than anything for Amy to know that she still had a mother.

Amy's mother, Wes thought as he sat in the rocker in his bedroom watching dawn color the walls. His arms were securely wrapped around his sleeping daughter, who had awakened crying during the night. He had brought her into his room and rocked her until she fell back to sleep. They had both struggled with the lonely void left in their lives since Patrice had died, and they were just beginning to get past the pain. But times like this, when disaster struck and fears and worries threatened to overwhelm him, Wes missed her most of all.

Closing his eyes, he rested his chin on Amy's head and reached with his heart toward the only true source of comfort he knew.

"Please protect my little girl, Lord," he whispered. "She's had so much pain."

Tears rolled down his face, and he looked helplessly up, as though he could see right through the ceiling into heaven. As though it had been poured into him, he felt a terrible compassion for the woman who'd been pregnant at eighteen, and spent the next seven years wondering about her child.

"Take care of Laney," he whispered. "Give her peace. Let her know she did a good thing by giving Amy to us."

He looked down at his daughter, her sweeping fringe of black lashes, her full, pink lips, her trailing black hair that his wife had rarely cut, her dark complexion. Amy would grow up to look exactly like Laney, he thought. She would be beautiful.

The telephone rang, and he picked it up before a second ring could disturb Amy. "Hello," he said quietly.

"Mr. Grayson, this is Laney Fields."

He swallowed and didn't answer.

"I'm sorry to call you so early, but I'd like to meet you somewhere this morning. I've been thinking, and we need to talk."

He hesitated. "I thought we'd covered everything."

"I'd still like to meet you."

Wes tightened his hold on his daughter, as if that would keep them both safe. "What about?"

"About Amy, of course."

She's changed her mind, he thought, his heart collapsing. His hand instinctively stroked Amy's arm. "You said I'd never see you again. You said—"

"I know what I said, Mr. Grayson," Laney whispered. "But there were things I didn't know then."

"Things?" he asked, his lips tightening. "What kinds of things?"

"I'd rather discuss this in person," she said. "Can we meet somewhere at ten o'clock?"

"I have a daughter," he bit out. "When you're a parent you can't just pick up and leave when you want to. I'll have to get a baby-sitter."

She was silent for a moment, letting him know she had felt the blow. "Will you be able to meet me or not?"

"All right," he said, realizing she wouldn't stop tormenting him until he did. "I'll get a baby-sitter and meet you at ten. At Brittany's Cafe on Third Street." He heard her hang up, listened for the dial tone, and stared at the receiver. She *had* changed her mind, he thought with a climbing sense of panic, just like he knew she would.

But if it cost him every ounce of strength he had, he would not let Laney Fields disrupt the life he had maintained for his child.

Laney sat in the quiet restaurant scanning the Saturday-morning diners, who spoke in soft tones about seemingly insignificant things. Hanging plants colored the atmosphere, and soft music gave the impression of peace. Laney was anything but relaxed. A shredded napkin lay before her, tiny pieces of evidence that, within, her emotions were at riot.

She saw Wes Grayson through the glass doors before he walked in. Quickly she gathered the shreds into a pile and wadded it up. It wouldn't do to let him know just how distressing this conversation would be for her, she thought. As calmly as she could manage, she lifted her coffee cup to her lips and peered at him over the rim. She saw him single her out and start toward her. His face was as pale as it had been yesterday, and his eyes were as red and tired as hers.

"Morning," he said when he reached the table.

Laney offered a wan smile, and he pulled out the chair next to her and sat down, a wary expression tightening his features.

"Have you eaten?" she asked.

"No," he said, setting his elbows on the table and clasping his hands in front of his face.

"Want to?"

"No," he said again with growing impatience. "Somehow I get the feeling I won't have much of an appetite in a few minutes." His eyes locked with hers, deep, searching, and when she couldn't deny the observation, he picked up the salt shaker and seemed to study it. "If you don't mind, I like directness. Why don't you get to the point?"

Laney shifted in her chair and folded her shaking hands in her lap. "There's no need for hostility, Mr. Grayson. We have a lot in common, whether we like it or not."

"We have nothing in common," he threw back. "Absolutely nothing."

"You adopted my daughter," Laney said.

"She's my daughter," he volleyed. "Has been since she was three days old. You don't have a daughter."

The beginnings of anger heated her neck. "I'm her mother," Laney said. "That may be difficult for you to grasp——."

"You gave up the right to be her mother when you let us adopt her," he interrupted savagely. "You should have thought about your maternal status seven years ago. It's too late now."

Laney looked down at her coffee, struggling to keep her voice low. "I wasn't given the luxury of thinking about it."

Wes didn't know what that meant, so he ignored it. "You gave her up, and we became her parents." He sighed at the pain in her eyes, and bending his head forward, he pinched the bridge of his nose. She was the enemy, he told himself, and Amy was their battleground. But it wasn't any easier for Laney than it was for him. He allowed himself a second to consider her feelings, her despair, her loss. "Look," he said in a softer voice. "I understand about regrets. And I'm not trying to be insensitive. From where I stand you did a good thing by giving her up if you weren't emotionally or financially capable of raising her."

"I was capable," Laney whispered. "I was then, and I am now."

The vein in Wes's temple began to throb visibly, and compassion for her position fled. "Don't threaten me, Laney. You can wipe that idea right out of your head because you're not getting her back." He realized he was drawing the attention of other diners and lowered his voice again. "You told me yesterday that you wouldn't make any claim on her. 'Take my word for it,' you said."

Laney took a deep breath and closed her eyes. "I know. And I meant it yesterday. But that was before you told me your wife died." She opened her eyes again and saw the deep pain illuminating his own eyes. "I know it still hurts," she conceded. "And I'm not trying to be insensitive, either. But it makes a difference in all this. A child needs her mother."

"Her mother is dead," Wes growled.

"No, she isn't. She still has a mother. She doesn't have to be deprived anymore."

"You're crazy," he whispered. "You're a complete stranger to her, and you think you can waltz into her life and pick up where her mother left off? No one can replace Patrice to her, but she's adjusting. I can give her what she needs."

"No, you can't," Laney asserted. "I don't believe that a man can be both mother and father to a little girl. A man is not able to give her all the emotional support she needs."

"What do you know about parenthood?" His harsh whisper whipped across her like a physical blow.

"Nothing. But I know about childhood. My mother died when I was nine, and my father had to raise me. I suppose he did the best he could, but it was sadly lacking. I don't want my child being raised that way."

"All right," Wes said, tossing his napkin aside. "So spit it out. What's the bottom line here?"

Her face reddened, and she struggled to hold back her tears. "I just want to meet her. I want to be involved in her life, to visit her when I want, to be there for her when she needs me."

Wes's expression hovered between violence and helplessness. "That's absurd," he said. "She doesn't even know you; how could she need you? She's been through a rough time in the past year, and I will not make her more insecure by bringing some stranger into her life who claims to be her real mother."

"You know I'm her real mother. You saw the papers."

Wes threw a quick glance at a passing waiter and made a valiant effort to keep his voice low. "But *she* doesn't know. Motherhood goes deeper than biology. It has very little to do with whose womb a child was carried in. It has to do with being there to celebrate an *A* on her report card and nursing her through the chicken pox and knowing the names of her best friends at school. It has to do with comforting her when she wakes up afraid in the middle of the night, with loving her and protecting her from unnecessary heartache. I can be her mother, too, if she needs one. She doesn't need you."

The pain his words inflicted was multiplied when Laney let herself consider what this was doing to Wes. He'd lost his wife, and now he feared losing his daughter. To him she was like a live grenade in his pocket, and she didn't want to be that. But it was for Amy that she went on.

Laney's eyes were soft and compassionate when they locked with his, and beneath the pain they held the dull gloss of strength gained from years of struggle. "Don't make me take you to court, Mr. Grayson," she said quietly. "Please. Amy has a mother, so there's no excuse for making her live without one for the rest of her life."

Wes's eyes were desperate. "You'd do that? You'd take me to court and upset her life that way?"

Laney leaned forward on the table, intent on making him understand. "I would never hurt her. She's my little girl too," she whispered. "I just want to know her, and I want her to know me. It doesn't have to be complicated."

Wes tilted his head helplessly, and a long, heavy breath escaped him.

"It's the most complicated thing in the world to Amy!" He coiled his hand into a fist and stared at it, then took a breath that only tied the knots tighter in his chest. "She's just a little girl. I don't want her traumatized."

Laney's resolve fell a degree. "Do you really think she will be?"

Wes brought his eyes back to hers and held them for a transparent moment. If only she didn't care, he thought, he could manage to detest her. But when she grew vulnerable and concerned, he lost his stand. Their heartaches and fears were pitted against each other. Who hurt the worst? Who feared the most? But Amy's pains and fears were all that mattered. "I honestly don't know," he whispered in answer to her question.

Laney cleared her throat and considered the alternatives. "Well, if you think it's too soon to tell her who I am, then maybe you could just introduce me as a friend. Maybe that would be better the first time, anyway. I'd be happy just to meet her and talk to her."

"Yeah," Wes mumbled. "Like you were happy just to see her and then to take her picture. You'll want more and more. The next thing I know you'll be tearing her up by telling her that you've decided to start playing mother."

"I *am* her mother," Laney said.

"I think it's a bad idea."

"Obviously."

Wes swallowed the lump in his throat. This wasn't getting them anywhere. The stakes were life-sized, and neither of them would surrender. All she wanted was a meeting. A simple ten-minute meeting under his supervision. It wasn't a lot to ask, and yet she might as well have asked him to cut off his hand. His chest seemed to constrict tighter. What choice did he have, after all? If he didn't cooperate, she might get more aggressive and get a lawyer. And maybe if he did cooperate, she'd back off and lose interest after a while. Maybe it was the novelty, the adventure, the impossibility of the situation that intrigued her.

His face was white as he brought his dull eyes to hers. "This afternoon at three," he grated out, as if he were handing her the weapon with which to wound him. "In the park."

Before Laney had the chance to thank him, he stood up and started for the door, his steady gait belying the anguish she had just inflicted on him.

Once outside, Wes slammed his truck door and collapsed against the steering wheel, wondering what he'd done to deserve having his world ripped apart in every conceivable way. He turned the key and the engine rolled over, then died. Pumping the gas, he tried again. Reluctantly, it started. Weary, he let it idle for a moment until he was sure it would get him out of the parking lot. Laney had more aces up her sleeve than she knew. If this came to some kind of court battle, how was he going to pay a lawyer's bill? He hadn't yet finished paying the hospital bills for Patrice's surgeries and chemotherapy, and there was a judgment against his home and his business. If he didn't manage to pay them off soon, he'd lose it all.

And now he faced the possibility that this woman might not stop at a mere introduction. She might want to go all the way with this.

He'd simply find a way to fight her, if it came to that. Maybe he could sell his truck and buy an even older model. And he could sell some of his furniture. If he managed to keep his house from the grips of the collectors, maybe he could sell it to pay for a lawyer.

He pulled out of the parking lot and slammed the heel of his hand against the steering wheel. It wasn't fair that Amy might have to lose her home on top of everything, as if the memories they had there had never taken place, as if Patrice's years with them had been a fantasy. He hoped he wouldn't wake up one day to find that his years with Amy were the same. Trials were given to make God's children stronger, he knew, but this trial was too much. God would intervene, wouldn't he? He wouldn't take Amy from him and thrust her into the undeserving arms of a stranger, would he?

His truck picked up speed and he turned on the stereo, adjusting the volume to a level intended to numb the mind, but still he thought. Still he remembered.

His days of childlessness came back to him, the years of praying, wishing, planning for a baby, the day they received the verdict that they could never have their own children, the long year of waiting after they had gotten on the adoption list. And he remembered the day the phone call came. They had felt like Abraham and Sarah when they'd learned they were having Isaac. But Wes and Patrice had been granted a girl, such a precious, cherished gift, with a head full of black hair and a tiny body that fit perfectly in the crook of his arm. He remembered how worried he'd been while she slept those first weeks, how he'd checked her breathing every few minutes, how he'd held her until she expected it every waking moment. He remembered the night when he and Patrice had lifted her up to God and dedicated her to him and promised that they would be faithful with this treasure he'd given them. He only wished he had Abraham's faith now and that he had the strength to face the possibility that God might demand such a drastic sacrifice of him.

"Don't ask this of me, Lord," he cried. "Please. Amy deserves so much better."

But maybe it wasn't God asking, he thought, and the Lord certainly knew how to protect his children. God knew that he could not have loved a child of his own seed more than he loved that little girl.

Swallowing back his worries and frustrations, he pulled into his driveway, wishing his trials had given him more faith. But he felt as frightened and uncertain as if he'd never experienced his Father's love.

And all he could see ahead of him was despair.

CHAPTER FOUR

From where she stood at the edge of the park, Laney saw Wes Grayson slumped on the bench, watching his daughter engaged in a game of kickball. She glanced anxiously down at the white jumpsuit she had chosen. Was it right? she wondered once again. What did one wear, after all, to meet one's seven-year-old daughter for the first time? What if Amy hated it? What if Amy hated her?

Ignoring the ache of threatening tears behind her eyes, she flipped her hair back over her shoulder, lifted her chin, and started toward Wes. She had loved ladies with long hair when she was a child, so she had let hers hang freely today. Now she wondered if it made her look too young. How would Amy relate to someone who looked like a kid claiming to be her mother?

She caught herself and forced back the hope that Amy would eventually learn who she really was. Wes had agreed to let her *meet* Amy, not spill out her heart.

She had no right to expect miracles, she thought as she walked toward him. She had given up on miracles long ago. The most she hoped for now was a chance.

Wes didn't move when she reached him. "She's playing kickball right now," he muttered without glancing at her. "We'll have to wait until the game's over."

"Of course." Laney swallowed and sat down next to him. She saw Amy kick the ball and run after it, then gasped when the black-haired girl tripped over a rock and caught herself.

"I'm OK, Daddy!" she shouted with a wave.

He waved back, then regarded Laney with a quick, dispassionate look.

Her cheeks stung, her nerves were frazzled, and her hands trembled like leaves rustled by an unforgiving wind. "She looks just like me," she said in a raspy voice.

Wes nodded, as if the concession was too much to make verbally.

His silence was as smothering as her fear was strangling, and if she could not relieve the fear, Laney resolved at least to break the quiet. "Thank you for letting me come," she said.

He moved his unfocused eyes back to the playground. "Didn't have much choice."

Laney regarded the austerity in his eyes, the dark circles beneath them, and the stubble darkening his jaw. "You had one."

A brief surge of guilt shot through her at the brooding shrug of his brows, but then she looked back at her laughing child and realized that her cause was a sound one, in spite of the pain it caused Wes Grayson.

The pain it caused within her, however, was something she hadn't expected. Giggles rolled over one another as Amy ran after the ball and kicked it, then took off in a sprint with the others. But the child's joy only widened a sorrowful fissure in Laney's heart. All the time lost. All the smiles missed. All the discoveries and the heartaches and the tears . . . they were gone forever, and all Laney had of them were a few brief memories of a tiny infant and some pictures she had had to hide in the shadows to take. "I held her, you know."

"What?"

"When she was born. They handed her to me . . ."

Laney felt his eyes burning into her with an appraisal teetering between burgeoning hostility and grudging sympathy. She told herself to stop before she broke down, but somehow it was important for him to know. "I watched her color change from purple to pink, and she held her head up just a little, and she had so much hair . . ." Her voice broke off, and she took a cleansing breath.

Wes looked away and squinted, unseeing, at something across the park. "Was that the last time you saw her?" he asked without inflection.

The sound of laughing children and passing cars and whispering leaves kept her control from snapping completely. "No," she said.

"I held her once more the next morning. I even nursed her . . ." She swallowed and pushed at the corners of her eyes, as if the pressure could dam the tears.

The ball escaped the players and rolled in front of them, and Wes gave it an absent kick toward the children. He looked back at her, his eyes effectively guarded. "I didn't know they let you hold your baby when it was going up for adoption."

"They usually don't," she said. "But I didn't plan to give her up."

A cloud gave way to sunlight, and a ray of it illuminated Wes's frowning face. He set his foot down and straightened out of his slump. Leaning forward and clasping his hands between his knees, he asked, "So why did you?"

Laney swallowed hard and brushed away the tear paving a path down her cheek. "Because my father was very insistent." She gave a sad laugh. "He had lots of reasons, among them the fact that I wasn't competent as a human being, much less as a mother. He said I would ruin her life."

"And you believed him?"

Laney met his gaze. "When you hear something enough you can't help believing it. And I was only eighteen. But that wasn't enough to make me give up my baby. I had an escape planned for the second day. I was going to take her and go as far away from my father as I could get. But he acted faster. When I went to get her she was already gone."

The lines around Wes's eyes deepened, as if the revelation somehow unsettled his own past. "But you must have signed something."

"After that I did," she admitted, looking back at the giggling little girl. "My father told me that I wasn't mature enough to make such a decision, and he was afraid I'd do something selfish instead of what was right. I felt defeated, so I signed."

She heard Wes clear his throat, and he looked away again, eyes narrowing further as he seemed to struggle with this new information. "What about Amy's natural father? Didn't he try to—"

Laney cut quickly across his question. "The only thing he tried to do was forget he'd ever known me. He reinforced what my father told me. And I believed them both."

41

A cloud veiled the sun again, casting shadows over the park, cooling the breeze a degree but not enough to account for the chill taking hold of her. Laney looked toward the playing children and wished she hadn't told him quite so much. She hadn't meant to burden him with her story. All she wanted was to meet her child.

Several moments ticked by as Wes seemed to digest her words. "What happened when you left the hospital?" he asked quietly.

Laney shrugged. "I left home after that and went to Houston. I never saw my father again." She stopped, tempered her voice. "I had time to grow up, time to learn my own value, time to find out that I wasn't a worthless burden, time to regret and wonder . . ."

"Time to decide to correct the bad hand you were dealt?" he asked, protective antagonism working back into his soft voice.

"I just wanted to make sure she was happy, to convince myself that things had worked out for the best," she said, unable to stop a new ambush of tears. "I thought then I could find peace and stop wondering if it was her every time I saw a little girl."

A mother and child passed by, and the child pointed at the tears staining Laney's face before being dragged away.

"I'm sorry," she whispered, dropping her face and letting her hair curtain her anguish. "I promised myself I wouldn't get emotional. That's not good for Amy."

Wes wet his lips and fought the compassion tugging at his heart. He lifted his hand to touch her . . . then pulled it back, fighting his own traitorous feelings. It wasn't easy to let a woman cry without comforting her, but he told himself that any sensitivity on his part might backfire. In many ways, she was the enemy.

"I . . . I just didn't want you to think that I'm some . . . callous monster."

"I didn't," he said. But his tone hovered somewhere between condemnation and compassion, as though he couldn't decide which to feel.

Forcing herself to get control, Laney wiped back the tears and dug into her purse for a tissue. She rubbed her face, ridding it of the evidence of tears, and glanced up at Amy, still playing ball. "She didn't see me crying, did she?" she asked anxiously.

Wes shook his head. "She's too busy."

Laney took a deep, shuddering breath and looked fully at her daughter laughing with her teammates, and realized her whole world hung on the smile of a small child. "I'm so nervous."

Wes followed her gaze, his own eyes glossing over, as if he didn't know which side to join in the battle of his feelings. "I'm a little nervous myself," he admitted. The wind ruffled his mahogany hair and made him look more endearing than she wanted to acknowledge. His full lips seemed to droop at the corners, and he stroked a knuckle across them.

"All this," she said, glancing back at the child, "and she probably won't even like me."

"She'll like you," he said in a quiet voice, but the words of assurance seemed to leave him without any for himself.

He looked back toward the children who were breaking up into smaller groups. "I'll go get her now."

"No!" The word came too abruptly but not as quickly as the dive of her stomach. She caught his hand.

He stopped and gave her a long, searching look that stripped her soul bare. "Why?"

"Because I'm scared."

Wes's throat convulsed, and he drew a breath that didn't seem to come easily. "It'll be all right, Laney."

The words comforted her more than anything else he could have offered, but his hard expression fought with the compassion in his voice.

"Will you stay?" she entreated anxiously.

"If you want me to," he said. "Just take it easy. I'll go get her." He stood up, but Laney grabbed his hand.

"Wes? Are . . . are you going to tell her who I am?"

His eyes were tormented when they meshed with hers, and he raked a hand through his hair. Finally, he whispered, "Not yet."

There was hope, she thought. He wasn't ruling it out forever.

But as Wes approached his daughter, he wasn't sure whether the little crumb of hope he'd thrown her was a form of self-betrayal or simple weakness.

"Daddy, they cheated," Amy told her father.

Wes slid his shaky hands into his jeans pockets and feigned a smile. "You always say that when you lose. Try being a good sport."

"I *was* being a good sport until they started cheating. They don't even know the rules."

Wes tousled her hair and wished that a meaningless game in the park was all Amy had to bring her down. "It's just a game, short stuff. Next time you can cheat."

A little smile broke through Amy's scowl. "You're not going to let me cheat."

Wes gave a shrug. "Well, maybe not. But that glimmer of hope might tide you over until next time."

Amy giggled and set her hands on her hips. "I'm not dumb."

Wes gave a mock gasp. "You're *not*? Then I'm going to have to rethink my parenting strategy a little."

"Daddy, you're so silly."

Wes feigned indignation. "Silly? I'll show you silly." With that he picked her up and threw her over his shoulder, tickling her until she squealed and twisted with delight.

"Let me down, Daddy!"

Wes gave in and let her down, her giggles lightening the weight of his burden a little. "Boy, you're heavy. What have you been eating?"

"Your cooking," Amy said with a smirk. "And it's made me *lose* weight."

"Don't insult my culinary talents, or I'll feed you oatmeal for the rest of the week."

Amy grimaced, and Wes stooped down and glanced toward Laney, who seemed to be loosening up as she watched the bantering with a look of poignant anticipation.

"Come on, short stuff. I want you to meet that lady over there."

Amy took his hand and followed him toward Laney. Wes watched Laney lean forward and give a shaky smile, a smile that touched his heart despite his efforts to ignore it.

When they were close to her, Amy offered her an astonished smile of recognition. "They let you out of jail, huh?"

Laney's face went blank, and she glanced up at Wes in a panic.

"For taking pictures," Amy continued. "Did they make you do push-ups?"

Wes rubbed his jaw and gave a slight grin as he sat down. "I think she has prison mixed up with spring training."

Laney found herself laughing with overwhelming relief, the first time she'd laughed since . . . she couldn't remember. "I didn't go to jail, Amy," she said. "And it's a good thing, because I'm hopeless when it comes to push-ups."

Wes pulled Amy onto his lap. "Honey, I told you they just asked her some questions. It was all a mistake. Laney and I are . . ." He hesitated on the word *friends*. "We know each other now, and she wanted to meet you."

Amy's tongue tested the hole where her front tooth had been as she pondered Laney. "Can you cook spaghetti?" she asked intently, as if that were an important clue to the woman's character. "Spaghetti that isn't runny?"

Laney's eyes sparkled as she smiled at the beautiful child. "Well, yes. I make very good spaghetti."

"Can you make it tonight? My daddy said he was feeding me oatmeal tonight."

"Oh, I don't know." Laney looked at Wes with uncertain eyes, suddenly embarrassed at the unexpected turn in the conversation. "He wouldn't really feed you oatmeal, would he?"

"Trust me," Amy assured her. "It's either that or canned soup. And he doesn't even warm it up right." A child across the park called her name, and her attention was diverted. "I have to go," she said quickly. "Sarah only has fifteen more minutes to play." With that she slipped out of her father's lap and barreled across the lawn toward her friend.

"Well," Laney said on a frustrated chuckle. "That didn't go exactly as I'd planned it."

"I think she liked you," Wes admitted. The words held a note of dread.

"For now," she said, casting him an uneasy glance, though relief danced in her black eyes. "I was intriguing to her. She thought I was an ex-con."

Wes almost smiled. "Yeah. Sorry about that."

"It's OK. It was a good icebreaker." Her big eyes sparkled, warming something inside him that had been cold a long time, and he told himself it was just because her eyes looked so much like Amy's.

"You're a good father. I can't imagine mine ever throwing me over his shoulder." A tendril of envy uncurled inside her . . . not just envy of Amy for having a father who cared but envy of the woman he had loved and married and made a family with. What was he like as a husband? she wondered fleetingly.

Wes's smile faded a degree, and he looked back at Amy. "If only playing and laughing were all it took to be a good father."

Laney followed his gaze and slipped the strap of her purse to her shoulder, leaning forward but not getting up, as if she didn't know whether to leave now or hang around until Amy's friend had gone.

Wes felt for her, in spite of himself, for she had suffered such emotional anguish to meet so little reward. And yet he didn't know if he was strong enough to offer her more.

Laney looked at him the same moment he looked at her.

"It was really—"

"You know, you don't—"

The sentences were begun simultaneously, then died off together. "Go ahead," they said together.

Black eyes locked mirthlessly with green ones, and finally Wes spoke. "She's expecting spaghetti," he said with a sober expression that told her the words were difficult. "And she wants you to cook it."

Laney felt warm blood coloring her cheeks, and she shook her head. "I . . . I couldn't impose that way."

Wes's eyes remained as serious as she'd ever seen them. "Cooking us dinner is no imposition," he said. "I'm not wild about my cooking, either."

Laney bit her lip and tried not to fantasize about the possibilities whirling through her mind. Making friends with her daughter, earning her love through a big dish of spaghetti, getting to know Amy's father . . . She cut her thoughts off with the last fantasy and searched for her voice. "I'd like that." She paused. "Could we tell her then?"

"We'll see," he said, and she wasn't sure if it was the thick clouds blotting out the sun or the utter fear of what was happening that had turned Wes's face pale. "Five-thirty?"

"Five-thirty," she agreed breathlessly.

At that moment, Laney almost believed in miracles again.

CHAPTER FIVE

Wes leaned against the counter in his tiny kitchen and watched Laney showing Amy how much oregano to sprinkle into the sauce. Except for his sister, Sherry, Laney was the first woman he'd had in this kitchen—in this house—since Patrice died.

He looked at his daughter standing on a step stool beside Laney, her black hair pulled up into a slightly crooked ponytail. She watched the sauce intently while she stirred. He knew that she missed her mother and that she missed the feminine guidance and instruction a little girl needed. And no matter how conscientious he was as a father, he would never be able to give her that.

"See, Daddy? It isn't runny," Amy told her father, holding up a spoonful. "Want a taste?"

"I'll wait," he said with a weak smile.

Laney glanced at him over Amy's head, a glance fraught with tension, and he realized he was inhibiting her. She had hardly been able to look at him all evening. It was as though their intense emotions mingled and multiplied when their eyes met. Where would this evening take the three of them? both pairs of eyes seemed to ask. And were the two of them, Wes and Laney, actually becoming friends?

Wes stiffened at the possibility and walked out of the kitchen asking himself why that would be so bad. Wouldn't it be easier for them to like each other and not constantly be at odds over what was best for Amy—if, indeed, she continued to insist on being part of their life?

The cramped den seemed more alive than it had in a year, simply because of the happy voices in the kitchen and the delectable smell drifting in the air. He sat down and stared at the scratched coffee table, marred with seven years of child's play. Even when they had been able to afford to replace it, Patrice had refused to part with it.

The scratches were a collage of memories, she had said. Teething marks and dropped toys and hard little baby shoes learning to climb. They had had so much happiness in this house, he thought, leaning back and resting his head against the couch. And so much misery.

Maybe Laney was right. Maybe Amy did need to know her birth mother. And maybe if he didn't make waves, Laney would be content with just visiting Amy when she wanted. Worse things could happen, couldn't they?

Amy darted out of the kitchen, holding her hands, smeared with butter, in the air the way a surgeon does after scrubbing. "Daddy, Laney let me make the garlic bread all by myself!"

"That's great, pumpkin," Wes said, trying to smile.

Amy leaned over him conspiratorially. "She's nice, isn't she?" she whispered.

"Yes. Very nice."

"And pretty too," Amy added.

Wes's smile dimmed a degree. "Pretty, too." Patting her behind, he turned her toward the kitchen. "Now go back in there and help her."

Amy scampered back into the kitchen, giggling like a child at the fair. "My daddy thinks you're pretty," she announced in a trumpeting voice.

Wes closed his eyes and vowed never to respond to one of Amy's baited questions again.

Laney couldn't escape the feeling of being granted a miracle at the way Amy responded to her. They were already friends, she marveled, and she felt amazingly comfortable with Wes. She looked up at him over her plate and noted that his tension had lifted a bit since they had sat down to eat. But still he wore that distant expression that told her a myriad of thoughts were clashing in his mind. He didn't want to like her, she realized. He probably resented the way she had fit so easily into Amy's heart. And he was probably still afraid.

He looked up at Amy and smiled at the careful way she coiled her spaghetti on her fork. He had a beautiful smile, Laney thought, and it looked as if he used it often. It was the kind of smile that came easily at the sight of his child, but it was also the kind of smile that made the sadness in his green eyes seem more pronounced. It must be hard to lose a spouse, she thought, looking back down at her food. It must be as bad as losing a child.

Amy took a dainty bite, but the minute she bit down the spaghetti exploded and drooled against her face. Wes laughed aloud, and Laney couldn't help smiling.

"Go ahead and slurp if you have to," he told his embarrassed daughter. "I don't think Laney'll change her opinion of you."

"Daddy, I can't," Amy whispered, mortified.

"I'll tell you what," Laney spoke up. "We'll all slurp. This business of having every piece of spaghetti in place is for the birds, anyway."

Amy watched, amazed, as Laney took a forkful of spaghetti and slurped it up. Laney dabbed her napkin over her mouth and looked at the two people gaping at her. "Well, am I going to do this by myself?"

Appreciation lit Wes's face, and for a moment the shadow faded from his eyes. "You heard the lady," he told Amy. "Start slurping."

They giggled through dinner and made a monumental fuss over the garlic bread Amy had made. But when the plates were empty, Wes's lightheartedness seemed to disappear as well. What would he do next? she wondered uneasily. Would he make her leave? Would he let her tell Amy who she really was? Or worse, would he leave the choice up to her, never giving his preference one way or another?

When he sent Amy to change into her pajamas, Laney stood up and reached for Amy's empty plate.

"Don't," he said, stopping her. "I'll clean up later."

"No," she argued. "Really, I want to."

"Then I'll help," he said, taking his own plate to the kitchen.

Laney wondered at the flock of butterflies in her stomach at the prospect of being left alone with him. Maybe he wanted to talk to her to ask her to leave quietly.

"You really don't have to do this." His voice came from behind her, too close to her ear, and she turned around. "The dishwasher's broken, and I haven't gotten it fixed. You can leave the dishes in the sink, and I'll do them later."

"I insist," she said.

"But you made dinner, so I should clean up. It's a rule Patrice and I . . ." His voice trailed off and he picked up the dish towel. "At least let me help," he said. "You wash, and I'll dry."

Laney looked at him for a moment. So many things she wanted to say, to ask. Would he think she was stepping out of line if she asked how Patrice had died? Would he want to talk about the woman who had loved both him and her child, or was the subject still too tender? Laney turned back to the sink and turned on the water.

When the squirt of soap transformed into a million suds, she started to wash the dishes quietly. He took the dishes from her one by one and dried them, then put them in the cabinets. An amused smile crept across his face, as if he'd thought of some private joke.

"What is it?" she asked.

"It's our system," he said, chuckling. "On *Sesame Street* they call this 'co-op-er-a-tion.'"

"Cooperation?" Laney asked, not quite seeing the humor.

Wes found her ignorance even funnier. "I guess you'd have to watch it."

"Guess so." Inept, she told herself. Trying to prove she could be a decent mother, and here she had never even watched *Sesame Street*!

Wes seemed to sober at the wistful look in her eyes, and she started to scrub harder. What would they talk about now? Would he ask her how she liked the weather? The silence was driving her mad, yet she couldn't think of an intelligent thing to say. Finally, groping, she said, "Amy's really smart for her age. She's amazing."

"Yeah, I guess it comes with being an only child. She's the center of attention around here. But you were an only child, weren't you?"

"Yes, but I wasn't the center of anything."

Wes let that sink in for a moment. "Tell me about your family," he said finally in a deep, quiet voice.

"My family?" It had never occurred to her that he would be interested.

One corner of his mouth rose. "You know, you're not the world's greatest conversationalist. You repeat everything I say."

Laney felt the color climbing her cheekbones. "Sorry. Guess I'm just a little nervous." She took a deep breath and worked at a burned place on one of the pans. "Why do you want to know about my family?"

He set a dry plate in the cabinet and took the wet pan from her hand. "I've wondered about Amy's grandparents. What kind of people were they?"

Ah, yes. They *were* Amy's grandparents, weren't they? Laney thought of her father. What could she tell him? That he was a shrewd, cold, calculating man who hadn't had a warm emotion in his body? No, she wouldn't tell him that. She'd tell him about the good things. She'd tell him about her mother.

"My mother was beautiful," she said softly. "She had that rare, mysterious kind of beauty that put women in awe of her and made men admire her. She was young when she married my father. Full-blooded Caddo Indian. To this day I find it hard to believe that my father would marry a stigma like that, but he did." She handed Wes a plate and picked up a pan. "She died when I was nine. I never knew her people."

"So it's true what the records said. Amy is . . . one-quarter Indian?"

Laney nodded. "Yes."

"You probably had to do a lot of fast growing up after your mom died, huh? Just like Amy."

Laney stared down at the pan in her hand. "Yeah, I guess so. Nothing was ever the same after that. I'm so sorry that had to happen to Amy, too. But you seem better than my father. Different."

Quiet settled between them for a few minutes before Wes asked, "You haven't told me much about your father. What did he do?"

Laney's features tightened. She pulled the drain in the sink and watched the sudsy water disappear. "He was a writer. He wrote political thrillers. Adam Fields."

The drying stopped and Wes's eyes darted to hers. "Adam Fields was your father? Adam Fields who wrote *Pacific Pride*?"

Laney kept her eyes on the drain. "Yes."

"He was famous."

"Yes, he was. His last book was on the *New York Times* best-seller list for forty-two weeks."

Was it pride in her voice or bitterness? Bitterness, probably, Wes thought, kicking himself mentally. She had already told him how her father had manipulated her. If he had any sensitivity at all, he thought, he wouldn't have asked.

He set the bowl in its place and turned back to her. She was still staring at the drain, running a weak string of water to rinse out the excess soap. What was she thinking? he wondered. Was she thinking of Amy or her father or him? Or was she considering whether they should tell Amy who she really was?

He reached for the wet colander she had set on the counter. It was too bad she looked so torn, he thought. It was too bad she smelled so sweet . . .

"Excuse me," he said softly behind her as he reached over her head to open a cabinet. His arm brushed briefly against her hair, and he withdrew it too quickly. The colander fell out of his grasp. Laney caught it at the same time he did. Too abruptly, she let it go and turned around, planning to slip out of his way.

Their eyes met, soot black ones holding glimmering green ones, and she held her breath. "The kitchen's too small," he whispered on an unsteady breath.

They stared at each other for what seemed another eternity, waiting, breath held . . . for what, neither of them seemed certain.

He looked at her lips and swallowed. "I don't think it will traumatize Amy to know you're her mother," he admitted finally. "Maybe it'll help her." After a fraction of a moment he added, "Maybe it'll help me."

A bubble of joy inflated inside her, joining the hope that had been growing all day. "Then we'll tell her?" she asked.

He nodded and stepped back. "We'll tell her," he said.

Then he left her alone in the kitchen, as if staying there with her meant relinquishing too much more of himself.

Amy had taken great pains to impress Laney in her choice of nightwear. She wore a long, pink flannel gown with long sleeves and a regal collar that Laney suspected would suffocate her if she stayed in it for long. The gown was obviously for winter, but it gave the little bright-eyed child a sense of royalty.

"You look like a little princess," Laney told her when she sat down on the couch across from her.

"That's what my mommy used to call me," Amy said. "Princess."

Laney's eyes darted to Wes, but he was looking pensively at Amy.

"Will you stay until I go to bed and tuck me in?" Amy asked Laney.

Laney smiled and looked at Wes for approval. He nodded that it was OK. "Of course. I'd love to."

Wes moved to the couch and pulled Amy into his lap. He wrapped his arms around her small waist and made her lean back against his chest. "Pumpkin, Laney and I want to talk to you about something. It's important, and I want you to listen very carefully."

Amy sat up on her father's lap, her face serious. "OK."

Laney felt a stir of emotion at the expression so close to fear on the girl's face. Was that how he'd led in to telling her that her mother was dead?

"Do you remember when Mommy and I told you about how you were adopted?" Wes began.

Amy nodded. "I remember."

He took a deep breath and looked at Laney again. "Well, we never talked much about the lady who was your mother before we adopted you, did we?"

Amy rubbed her nose and shook her head. "No. You said you didn't know who she was and that it didn't matter because I was yours."

Wes paused a moment, as if he didn't know how to go on. His gaze coasted to Laney, measuring her for the help he needed. It was there in her dark eyes, filling in strength where he had weakness, the way his wife had once done. Finally he turned Amy to face him in his lap, and he dropped his forehead against hers. "Well, I know who she is now, pumpkin. And I think it's time you knew her too."

Amy stiffened in his lap, a tiny frown clefting her brows. She drew back to look at him, as if she couldn't believe until she saw it in his eyes.

Laney set a hand on Wes's shoulder when she realized he couldn't go on. He looked at her mutely, his groping expression inviting her to take it from there. She scooted closer to them, closer to the warmth the two of them exuded as a family, closer to the circle of love that was foreign to her. Struggling not to let the fierce emotion overwhelm her, she looked at her daughter.

"Amy, the other day when your daddy had me arrested in the park, it was because he saw me taking pictures of you. I didn't mean any harm. I just wanted to see you. Ever since you were born and were taken away from me, I've wanted to see you."

The worry lines on the child's innocent face deepened, but she looked at Laney as if she still didn't quite grasp what she was being told.

Laney arched her brows emphatically and struggled to make the words clear. "Amy, I'm your mother."

Amy's black eyes widened guardedly, and a flustered color traveled up her cheeks. "No, you're not. My mother died."

"But I'm your re—" She caught herself on the word *real* and tried again. "I was your first mother."

The silence in the room was almost deafening, and the denial in the child's eyes was piercing. Would she love her when she believed? Laney asked herself. Would she invite Laney to fill the void her mother had left? When Laney thought she could take the suspense no longer, Amy turned to her father, the only anchor she had in the world, and whispered, "Was she, Daddy?"

Wes squeezed her more tightly. "Yes, baby."

Tears welled in the child's eyes, and Amy's bottom lip began to quiver. Her words were an octave higher than they had been before, revealing the terror in her bruised heart. "Are you going to give me back to her?"

Wes caught his breath, as if the question had scalded him, and framed Amy's face with his big, protective hands. "No." The word came out long and whispered. "It's you and me. We're a team."

Laney felt the joy within her deflate as if it had never existed, but the hope still bobbed precariously in her heart. She watched in misery as Amy slid her arms around her father's neck and buried her face into his chest. His expression became cold, almost vicious, as he held her. They had made a mistake, Laney thought frantically, and he was blaming her.

Amy pulled back, and Laney's stomach coiled into a million knots at the dull, resigned expression on her face. "I'm tired," the child said, climbing off her father's lap. "I think I'll go to bed. I don't need to be tucked in."

The words slashed at Laney's heart like a knife. But *she* needed to tuck her in and sing her a song and read her a story, Laney thought. Yet Amy's needs were more important. Laney felt the chilling rejection in the loneliest regions of her heart, but she refused to let the child see her cry. Amy was under enough pressure, enough stress, without having to deal with that. It was ironic, Laney thought. This was one of those times when Amy desperately needed a mother . . . except that the only mother she had left was responsible for her pain.

"Good night, Amy," Laney said.

Amy stopped at the door and turned back to Laney, her eyes bearing as much bitterness as seven-year-old innocence would allow. "I'm not going to call you Mother," she said defiantly.

"That's OK," Laney choked out. And as the little girl disappeared up the hallway like an elusive image in a dream, Laney felt as if her heart had been ripped out.

Wes's cold silence made things even worse. She dropped her face into her hands and gave in to a rending sob. When she thought she could speak again, she wiped her face and looked up at him.

His eyes looked weary, lifeless, as he stared in the direction Amy had gone.

"I'm so sorry, Wes," Laney said. "It was too soon. She wasn't ready. I should have seen—"

"I was afraid this would happen," he whispered miserably. "I shouldn't have told you to go ahead."

Laney took a few steps toward the door. "She needs someone, Wes. Don't leave her alone back there. She's so little . . ."

He nodded agreement but turned back to Laney. "Look, it was an experiment that failed. It's better if from now on you just stay away. I know it's asking a lot, but I don't want her traumatized."

Laney stood up to face him. Had she come so close only to lose everything? Was this just another trick that life had played on her? Dangling a treasure before her only to snatch it away, the way everything she'd ever wanted had been? No, she told herself defiantly. Amy needed her, whether she knew it or not, and Wes couldn't stop Laney from filling that need.

"Wes, I can't disappear now when she finally knows who I am. She'll think I abandoned her again!"

"You owe her some peace, Laney. She doesn't deserve all this."

Since her father had robbed her of her child, Laney hadn't felt such helpless frustration. She had pled with him too—and lost.

"Wes, please. She liked me. Even you had to see that."

"Well, she doesn't like you now," he said, growing angry. "And that's all that matters, isn't it? Now please, give me some time alone with her."

Laney got her purse and clutched it tightly against her stomach. She started out the door, unable to bear looking up at him.

Oh, hope could be such a cruel emotion, a mocking weapon. It took people at their most vulnerable and shattered them when they surrendered to it. Laney had let herself hope today for the first time in years. And in one fell swoop her fragile, newly constructed world had come crashing down. All it took was a child's denial. All it took was the frost in a pair of green, grieving eyes.

Neither the grief nor the anger had subsided a week later when Wes's sister burst into his office. "You're an idiot, you know that?"

Wes looked up from the books spread out on his desk and rubbed his hands over his tired eyes. "Leave me alone, Sherry," he told her as she leaned in the doorway with her arms crossed judgmentally. "I'm in a bad mood."

"Of course you're in a bad mood," she said, walking toward him, her abrupt footsteps jarring the walls of the tiny trailer they worked in. "You should be."

"I mean it, Sherry," he warned. "Don't provoke me today." He really didn't think he could take it. Ever since he had told her about Laney and the night she had made spaghetti, his sister had been hounding and badgering him.

"Provoke you?" Sherry said, pushing her shoulder-length, blond hair back from her face. "I ought to shoot you! You're digging your own grave, Wes. She called again!"

Wes's eyes snapped to attention and that wariness Sherry had grown so used to crept back into them. "I told you, I don't want to see her or talk to her."

She let out a disgusted breath and set her hands on her hips, trying to steady her voice. "Wes, Laney Fields is a very determined woman. She's getting impatient with you. I'm really worried about what she might do."

"Do you honestly think I'm not? Birth mothers file suit against adoptive parents every day. And sometimes they win, regardless of the best interests of the child."

Sherry sat down knee to knee with him. "Wes, if she does file suit, you don't have the money to fight it. But you could cooperate a little and avoid all of this."

Wes looked down at his books, at the figures that told him the office building his company was just finishing was way over budget, at the notices from hostile creditors breathing down his neck, at the hospital bills that would have broken a rich man. He had never been rich.

"Just let her see her again," Sherry said. "Just a harmless little visit."

"I can't cooperate at Amy's expense," he said.

"But, Wes, if she gets you in court and it comes out that you can't even pay your grocery bill these days, how do you think that'll look?"

His arm flailed across his desk, knocking the books and papers off with a loud clatter. "I have no choice!" he shouted, the tendons in his neck straining against the skin.

Sherry's silence was all the condemnation he needed for his outburst. He steepled his shaking hands in front of his face, and his eyes softened as he looked at his sister who had literally prayed him through the despair and depression in the toughest times of his life. Even now, she worked for him for free when she wasn't waiting tables or attending her fashion designing classes because he hadn't been able to pay his secretary. "I'll do what I have to do, Sherry."

"I'm just saying that maybe you have alternatives," she said quietly.

He dropped his head down and cupped his hands over the back of his neck. "Sherry, you don't have a child. You don't know what it's like."

"I have a niece," she reminded him.

He squeezed his eyes shut. *She's afraid I'm going to give her back to Laney. She doesn't understand, and she doesn't trust Laney.* "I can't make her spend Sundays at the zoo with a woman who threatens her security. I'd sell everything I have if I could keep Amy from getting hurt and being afraid."

Sherry only studied him for a long moment. Finally she leaned across his desk and dropped a kiss on his forehead. "And I'd sell everything I have to keep from seeing my brother so scared," she whispered. "But I don't have anything except a stack of IOUs for back pay and a little objective, unwelcome advice. One of these days you'll listen to me."

"One of these days," he agreed, looking up again, his sad eyes breaking her heart. "But not today."

Sherry straightened and gave him a regretful smile. "Then I'll keep telling her you're not available to take her call," she said. She started for the door, but Wes stopped her.

"Sherry?"

Sherry turned back to him, the beginning of a smile tugging at her lips.

"Thanks," he said.

"No problem," she answered, then closed him into the tiny office, alone with a million problems for which he had no solutions.

Laney sat in her car and propped her elbow on the open window as she gazed wistfully at the busy playground of Amy's school. After several days of watching, she had determined the time every day that Amy's class had recess. She had watched day after day, learning small details about her daughter that she hadn't known before. She knew that her two best friends were a little blond girl with a pixie haircut who followed Amy around like a shadow and the redhead named Sarah, who had played with her at the park. She knew which boys she liked to have picking on her from the way she smiled and fought back when one pulled her hair or tripped her. And she got to know a bit about Amy's teacher from the way she punished the rowdy children and slackened the reins on the behaved ones. What she didn't know, however, was whether Amy had come to terms with what she had learned and whether she would react with hostility or pleasantness when Laney confronted her again.

A deep chasm of sadness ached inside Laney, and she closed her eyes. It wasn't fair, she thought. Life was so cruel. The flicker of fear and dormant despair in Amy's wide eyes the night they'd told her came back to her. If the child had slashed a knife right through her heart, Laney couldn't have felt worse pain. She opened her eyes again and sought out her daughter drawing in the dirt with a stick. Why couldn't it have turned out differently? And why had the cold warning in Wes's voice when he'd made her leave been haunting her ever since? Why did the misery in his eyes keep her awake at night? Because he was a good man and she liked him, she told herself, and hurting him was the last thing she wanted.

"What am I going to do?" she whispered, not letting herself cry. If Wes wasn't a gentle, caring father, if he wasn't so capable, if the only happiness she'd seen in him hadn't been tied up in that little girl, she would have been in court in a flash. If that sparkle of vulnerability, that guarded hurt-me-but-not-my-daughter look, that expectation of pain for both of them didn't shine so apparently in his eyes, she might have been able to decide what to do. Why wouldn't he take her calls? Why couldn't they at least discuss it?

She watched as Amy's teacher strolled out toward the playing children and sat down on a bench. Amy ran to her and tugged on her sleeve. Her teacher, a good-natured, older woman, put her arm around Amy's shoulders as the girl chattered up at her.

A woman's touch. Laney was glad she was getting it somewhere. But who would Amy turn to once school was out?

She wondered if Wes really did have what it took to raise her alone. Laney's own father certainly hadn't. She had learned very young that tears were only tolerated in the privacy of her bedroom with the door closed. She'd gotten random hugs from housekeepers and neighbors, and, like Amy, from teachers. But it was far from enough.

Amy needed a mother. And no matter how nurturing and caring Wes could be, at times all the good intentions in the world fell short. Times when the girl would cry out in the night for a mother, perhaps not even knowing herself that that was what she cried for. Laney wanted to be there when she did and hold her and comfort her the way she had so needed to be comforted as a child. She wanted her daughter to know where she could always go for a woman's hug.

Laney watched the children being called back into the school building, and she started her engine, the noise grating across her consciousness like a chain saw. She and Wes had known destruction, and they both knew the dark, drastic feeling of loneliness. It had to end somewhere, she thought. She had no intention of taking Amy away from Wes. But if she had to use the court system to get regular visitation, she might as well try for what she knew would be better for her child. She knew that a custody battle would rip Wes apart. She even knew that it might hurt Amy—in the short run. But in the long run, she convinced herself, it would be for the best. In the long run, Amy needed to have both a father—*and* a mother. That way, they could both be there for Amy.

One of them would have to take the chance to make them all winners in a situation that spelled loss by its very nature. One of them would have to look ahead instead of behind. And someday they would all stop hurting.

CHAPTER SIX

Two months later—two months that had crept by with a new kind of cruelty—Laney finally sat in the courtroom, staring down at her clenched hands on the table in front of her. Though she had seen Amy often from a distance over the last several weeks, she hadn't seen Wes. Now she could see the toll this was taking on him. He had lost weight, the lines in his face were more pronounced, and he moved like a man with a hundred pounds of dread weighing his shoulders down. Since he had walked in, Wes had not looked at her. His eyes were dull and fixed on the table in front of him, as if he could keep his control only if he kept his eyes steady. He looked tired, and the lines branching out from his eyes seemed more deeply etched than they had before. He wore creased black pants and a gray jacket that fit his tall frame well. The missing button on the jacket told her it was not new, however.

Absently she smoothed back her sleek chignon and straightened her beige blazer. It was hot in the room, even though a ceiling fan buzzed overhead. Like Wes, she had to sit there and listen as her lawyer presented all the evidence they had—indisputable evidence in the form of documents, blood tests, and photographs—proving she was the child's mother. And then, just as she'd expected, Wes's lawyer presented his documents showing that Amy had been legally adopted, presenting Laney's signature on the papers with great emphasis.

The room grew hotter, and tiny beads of sweat glistened on Wes's forehead. Laney watched her lawyer pace across the room as he drilled Wes's character witnesses: his sister, his best friend, his neighbor. With great interest her lawyer dwelt on the fact that Amy had not been taken for either her six- or seven-year checkups. The man was shrewd and missed nothing. That was why her father had used him for all his business. They had the same impenetrable temperament, the same go-for-the-throat strategy, the same conviction that the end always justified the means. He was the same lawyer who had drawn up Amy's adoption papers, the same man who had told Laney where to sign on the dotted line, who had patted her hand and praised her for her "mature" decision. But he had known that the decision was not Laney's. And that was why she had hired him to represent her. Perhaps his guilt would make him try harder, she thought. Perhaps his shrewdness would give them an edge. Perhaps his experience with this judge would weigh in their favor.

When the last of the character witnesses was dismissed, John LaRoux, her attorney, clasped his hands behind his back. "Your honor, I'd like to call Wesley Grayson to the stand."

She watched Wes's throat convulse as he stood up and started to button his coat, then remembered the missing button and let it go. His shoulders stiffened as he took the stand, and his alert eyes narrowed against LaRoux's missile-like questions.

The missiles were expertly aimed and just as destructive. Laney listened with disbelief as her attorney drilled him in a mocking voice about his financial state, about the fact that he'd declared a loss on his income taxes for the preceding year, about the judgments against his home and his business, about the bills that Wes still hadn't been able to pay off.

"I'm self-employed," Wes said in a shaky voice, trying desperately to restrain his anger. "My health insurance costs a fortune, and it doesn't cover much. When my wife got sick . . ." His voice cracked, and he stopped and steadied himself. Swallowing, he started again. "There were a lot of expenses, and my insurance didn't cover much at all. I had to pay for most of it. It set me back a little."

"A little?" LaRoux echoed. "Exactly how much do you still owe, Mr. Grayson?"

Wes glanced at his lawyer. The man gave him a nod, telling him to go ahead.

"Somewhere around thirty-five thousand dollars," he said quietly.

"Do you have any hope of paying that off, Mr. Grayson?" LaRoux asked.

Wes looked at the judge, then at Laney. "I'm doing the best I can."

"And does your 'best' include possible bankruptcy?"

Wes took a beat too long to answer. "I don't know." He took a deep breath and tried to explain. "I have several bids out, and I'm working on one for the new amusement park project. I might be able—"

"But no contracts?"

"Not at the moment. We just finished a project, but it was over budget because of some problems that came up—"

"Thank you, Mr. Grayson," LaRoux said, cutting him off. The attorney smiled and turned to the judge, but Laney's eyes remained on Wes. His jaw tensed as he stared at the floor, bracing himself for what he knew was to come. His eyes were opaque, but behind the dullness was fear so great that it made Laney shiver. The man had lost more than his wife. He had almost lost his business and his home, he had gone into debt so great that he had little hope of ever getting out from under it, he faced the prospect of losing his daughter, and now he was losing his dignity as well.

Her eyes darted to her lawyer's, and she wondered where he'd gotten his information and what bearing he thought it had on this case. Surely he didn't think that a lack of money made Wes a poor father. That wasn't what she'd wanted to prove. All she wanted was to have her own place in Amy's life, without hurting Wes in the process.

"Your honor," LaRoux went on in a bored voice. "It's apparent that this man is under a great deal of stress, financially and otherwise. He hasn't even had the money to take his child for her checkups—"

"I take her to the doctor when she's sick!" Wes blurted, his face reddening.

"Your honor," the attorney went on, as if Wes's outburst was irrelevant, "a man in this much debt has to cut corners. Where does he cut them? With the child's clothing, food, medicine?"

"I object!" Wes's lawyer said, and Laney breathed a sigh of relief.

Laney wanted to object as well. She hadn't done this to humiliate Wes Grayson and strip him of his dignity. She'd never said he neglected Amy! She half rose in her chair, trying to get her attorney's attention and stop him, make him take back what he'd said on her behalf, make him give Wes back his pride. When her attorney ignored her furious eyes she sank back down.

What had she done?

The objection was sustained, but LaRoux had other aces up his sleeve. "We're talking about a little girl. A little girl in a home with a man who can hardly support her, a man who may not even be able to keep a roof over her head, a man with a failing business to run, a man who isn't even her natural father."

Wes's eyes snapped to Laney's and locked with them. *How could you do this to us?* they asked.

She arched her brows helplessly and shook her head. Had she really paid that man to drive a wedge between her and her daughter's father, to ruin any chance of her ever being friends with him, to drive out the last remnants of his self-respect?

The nightmare would not end until it was played out. "On the other hand," her attorney went on, "we have my client, a woman wealthy from her father's inheritance, a woman who cared so much for the child once already that she made the decision to put it up for adoption in hopes that the adoptive parents could give it a better life than she could have at eighteen."

His daughter was not an "it"! Wes wanted to scream. He bit his lips to keep the words back, and his nostrils flared.

"How could she have known that the adoptive mother would die and that the child would be left with a man with so many problems that . . ."

Wes's hand coiled into a fist in his lap, and his face was tinged with scarlet. This wasn't happening, he told himself. The judge was smarter than that. He would realize Amy was the most important thing on earth to him.

Laney dropped her face into her trembling hands. *Leave him alone!* she mentally railed.

But LaRoux would not be cut short.

" . . . is only asking for a joint custody agreement. My client doesn't wish to traumatize the child by taking her from her father, nor does she wish . . ."

He was losing, Wes thought, a smothering wave of panic washing over him. Strangers were making a decision that was going to change Amy's life.

Laney stood up, her chair scraping on the cold tile floor. The judge's attention left the attorney, still in the midst of his diatribe, and went to her. Wes looked up. LaRoux wheeled around.

"Your honor, I apologize for interrupting, but may I please have a word with my attorney?" she asked tersely.

LaRoux's eyes were glinty beads of steel as he stepped toward her, warning her that he wouldn't tolerate such behavior. "What do you think you're doing?" he asked in a whisper.

"I'm stopping you," she hissed. "You've gone far enough. We could have made our point without ruining Wes Grayson. He's a good father and a kind man, and I won't sit here and pay you to kick him in the teeth."

LaRoux's spine stiffened. "Exactly what would you like me to do?"

"Dismiss him from the stand," she said. "And leave him alone."

As LaRoux turned slowly back to the judge, Laney tried to steady her furious, heaving breaths. Her eyes went back to Wes's, and she noted that they were a little softer in their reproach. Had he realized what she was telling her attorney?

She watched as Wes was dismissed, and the judge slipped to his chambers for a few minutes. It would take only a few minutes, she thought miserably. A few minutes to give her back her daughter— and possibly destroy Wes Grayson.

When LaRoux walked back to the table his eyes glowered. "You've got it in the bag," he said as he stuffed papers into his briefcase, "despite your efforts to go on being a loser."

"No one had to lose!" she whispered. "I could have gotten joint custody without attacking him. I had enough of an argument, and you know it. I wanted it to be fair."

"It's only fair if you win," he said.

"You don't care who gets hurt, do you? You don't see this as affecting human lives or hurting decent people."

"Do you?" the cold attorney asked. "If I recall, you said that the child hadn't even welcomed you into her life." He uttered a dry, brittle laugh. "You hired me to hurt those decent people, so don't give me the self-righteous routine now that I've gotten you what you wanted."

Laney stared at him as he lowered to his seat, and slowly her angry, guilty eyes drifted to Wes. For a moment she wished she could take it all back, start over, and find some other way. Their eyes met for a split second before he turned away, and she felt colder than she'd ever felt in her life.

The judge returned to the courtroom ten minutes later, his judicial robe brushing the floor as he walked to the bench. Making a production of shuffling the papers on his desk and adjusting his glasses, he prepared to give his answer.

"After reviewing this case thoroughly . . ."

Wes clasped his hands in front of his mouth and closed his eyes. *Please, God*, he prayed. *Prove that there's still justice in this world . . .*

Laney coiled her fingers in her lap and set her eyes on the judge.

Both held their breath. Both sweated. Both died a little inside as the judge grew long-winded, recounting both sides of the issue.

And then he finally said, "And for that reason, I award Ms. Fields joint custody of her daughter."

Laney caught her breath in a sob, momentarily forgetting all the pain and sorrow it would cause the man at the table across from her.

Wes drew in an agonizing breath and wondered why he felt surprised, why he felt cheated, why he felt betrayed when he had expected it. He dropped his forehead into his hands. How was he going to tell Amy? He looked up, his green eyes indicting as they met Laney's anxious ones. Her joy instantly faded, and guilt flashed through them.

The judge finished his statement, and court was adjourned. Laney pushed past the attorneys and made her way toward him, trying—and failing—to look as if she understood what he was going through.

"Wes," she said before he could rebuke her. "Please. I didn't mean for any of those things to come out. I didn't know them myself."

Wes started out of the courtroom, his brisk pace making her trot to keep up.

"My attorney was cruel," she said, "and you know I don't believe you've neglected Amy in any way. That wasn't the point—"

"Then what *was* the point?" he asked, swiveling abruptly, almost making her run into him.

"I just wanted to have a part in her life. You wouldn't let me see her."

His nostrils flared, and for a moment she thought he might break down before her. But when his words came out they were steady and calculated. "I won't force her to go with you," he warned in a deadly quiet voice. "Before I'll let you destroy her, I'll take her so far away you'll never see her again. I'd tread lightly if I were you."

Tears sprang to Laney's eyes. "Wes, please give me a chance," she whispered.

He turned and walked away.

Wes was proud of himself. He had managed to drive home without running into any cars, without driving off an embankment, without slamming into any brick walls. He had not self-destructed.

He walked into his empty house and dropped his keys on the telephone table. He still had an hour before Amy got home from school. One hour to fall apart and put himself back together again.

His bedroom was dark, and he went in and sat on the bed— Patrice's side—and gazed at the eight-by-ten picture of her he kept on the nightstand. He clutched his arms across his stomach and doubled over as the agony deep in his soul bubbled to the surface. Wilting, he lay on the bed on her pillow. "Patrice," he cried, as tears squeezed out of his eyes.

His voice made the darkness darker, the loneliness lonelier. He grabbed the pillow from under the bedspread and clutched it against his chest. "I miss you," he whispered as he wept.

He didn't cry for long. His tears reached deep inside and tore great chunks from what was left of his heart. When he was spent he lay on his back still clutching the pillow and stared at the ceiling.

What would he do when Amy was with Laney? He couldn't bear to come home to this empty house, to sleep without checking on her at night, and to wake without her early-morning smiles and her childish demands for things she knew he wouldn't let her have for breakfast. The loneliness would kill him. Yet there was nothing he could do.

Was it his destiny to love only for a while and never learn to say good-bye?

Laney sat in the frilly bedroom she had decorated for Amy and looked at the pink and white dust ruffle beneath the soft pink comforter, at the subdued wallpaper, and at the French Provincial furniture that had been delivered the day before. Would Amy like what she had done to this room? she wondered. Would she see the love that had gone into it? Would she feel the warmth that Laney knew she could give her?

She pulled her feet up on the bed and folded her arms over her knees. Her daughter. Her baby. Was life finally making itself up to her, or was she setting herself up for a fall?

No, she thought. There was no room for fear. She would look ahead to the talks they would have in this room, to the questions she would answer, and to the love they would exchange. She deserved that love. She closed her eyes and tried to picture Amy's exuberant smile and that long winter gown that transformed her from tomboy to princess.

Mommy, who was the first boy you ever liked?

There was a boy named Georgie who sat next to me in the second grade.

Did he pull your hair?

Every chance he got. And he wrote on me and threw dirt at me at recess and tied my shoelaces together . . . It was true love.

Mommy, why didn't you ever get married?

Laney opened her eyes to the empty room. "Because there was too much unfinished business, too many ties, too many questions," she whispered. "Because I could never move on with my life as long as I'd left you behind."

Her heart ached with the pain that had presided in her soul for so long. It would work, she told herself. It would work for all of them. Even Wes. Laney would make it work.

She closed her eyes and imagined the little girl tucked into the bed, smiling up at her. "I'll try to make it easy for you," she whispered to the absent child. "And for your daddy."

Quiet was all the response she got, leaving her with a cool, empty feeling that she expected to be temporary. When she had summoned all her strength, she pulled off of the bed and went to the telephone in the den. He'd be waiting for her call, she thought. Waiting fearfully, miserably for her to tell him when she wanted to take Amy. If only he could see how right this was, she thought, he would be happy.

The phone rang four times before a quiet, masculine voice answered. "Hello?"

"Hi," she said simply.

Silence.

"I thought we should talk about our schedule," she said. When he didn't respond, she went on, going through the speech she had rehearsed over and over in her mind. "If it's all right, I'd like to have her this weekend, and then I was thinking that I could keep her after school until you get home, so she doesn't have to stay with the baby-sitter. When school's out I could keep her during the day, and you could have her at night. That way, her life wouldn't be disrupted. When she's more used to me, we could alternate weekends and maybe work up to a night or two a week."

"And if it's not all right?"

She heard the anger vibrating in his voice. "Wes, it won't be ideal for either of us. It'll be hard for me to let her go at the end of the day."

"The sacrifices you're willing to make," he said sarcastically.

She swallowed the lump in her throat and forced herself to go on. "Tomorrow's Saturday. I want to pick her up at ten o'clock. I'll bring her back Sunday."

No answer.

"Look at the bright side," she offered. "You can date without getting a baby-sitter. You could go out tomorrow and—"

"I don't exactly feel like celebrating," he said.

She gave a limp sigh. "No, I don't suppose you do." An idea occurred to her, and her eyes found new life. "You could come over here for dinner tomorrow night. Make sure that everything's going well. It might make you feel better. Amy too. I think it's important for her to see us as friends."

"She knows we're not friends," he said.

"Still," she tried again, "we could try."

"I'll think about it," he said.

"Ten o'clock, then?"

"You're running this show."

She brought a shaky hand to her forehead. Why did he insist on making this so difficult? "All right. I'll see you both then."

The click told her he had hung up. She set the phone in its cradle and tried not to feel the anguish, the misery he was feeling. She tried to erase the image of haunted green eyes from her mind, tried to forget the defeated slump of his broad shoulders as he'd stormed out of the court building that afternoon. Friendship between them seemed impossible, and that was a shame because they needed each other tonight.

But tonight would be over soon enough, she thought finally. And tomorrow she would have Amy.

CHAPTER SEVEN

When he answered the door the following morning, Wes's eyes were tired and red and filled with an undisguised contempt Laney feared she would always see there. His brown hair was tousled, as if he hadn't yet thought to brush it, and his shirttail hung out over his jeans. Without greeting her, he stepped back and let her into the quiet house.

Laney smoothed her French braid with a trembling hand and stepped inside. Amy sat on the couch, staring down at her hands clasped in her lap like a little girl about to be taken to reform school for having done nothing wrong.

"Hi, Amy," she said cautiously.

Amy didn't answer.

Laney turned back to Wes. "Please," she mouthed, pleading for him to act civil, "for Amy's sake."

Wes took a deep breath and looked at his daughter. He wet his lips, as if he were about to speak, but nothing came out. After another visual entreaty from Laney, he sat down beside Amy.

"Your hair looks nice," he told Laney in a poor attempt at sounding friendly. "Maybe you can do that to Amy's hair. I'm not too good with things like that."

"Of course I can do hers," Laney said.

When Amy didn't respond, Laney returned her troubled eyes to Wes. Even through his dislike she saw his vulnerability, his plea for her to tread lightly, and the silent repetition of his wish of weeks ago: *I hope you're a decent person.* She reached out and touched his arm to reassure him. Amazingly he didn't pull away, and he didn't tense up. And for a fleeting moment Laney thought she would rather do anything in the world than hurt him.

"Will . . ." Her voice caught, and she cleared her throat and tried again. "Will you be coming for supper?"

Amy looked up at that, her big eyes pleading.

"Yes, I'll come," he said finally. Then, forcing a smile, he said, "I never miss a good home-cooked meal."

Laney arranged her smile so that Amy wouldn't see the turmoil within her. "Amy, did you pack your bathing suit?"

The child shook her head negatively.

"She doesn't have one," Wes said. "She's outgrown last year's, and we haven't gotten her another one."

"No problem," Laney said. "We'll go shopping and buy you one. I've always wanted to take you shopping."

Amy shrugged indifferently.

"Well, we'd better get going," Laney said. "Your dad probably has a lot of things to do."

"Yeah," he said miserably.

Amy stood up and got her small overnight case, then followed Laney to the front door. Wes walked behind them and opened the door. Amy headed for the car before Laney was out of the house.

Laney turned back to Wes, his arm propped on the doorjamb as he stared wistfully after Amy, his eyes wide and misty.

"You should get some sleep," Laney told him quietly. "She'll be fine."

His throat convulsed, and he nodded.

"Supper's at six," she added.

He couldn't answer. Somehow, Laney understood why. Turning, she followed her daughter to the car, hoping that things would take a turn for the better.

But they didn't. The shopping spree proved to be disastrous. Amy, who still refused to speak to her, showed no preference for anything and even declined to try on a swimming suit. Taking a guess at her size, Laney took a chance and bought one anyway.

Before they left the mall, which was busy with chattering Saturday shoppers, Laney led Amy to Baskin-Robbins for ice cream. But Amy found nothing to interest her. Even McDonald's had no appeal to the child, so Laney finally gave up and took Amy home.

The room would do it, she thought. When Amy saw that bedroom she would flip. It was every little girl's dream, and it had been custom decorated just for Amy. But when she led Amy through the big house and to her room, Amy didn't bat an eye.

"It was the way I wanted my room to look when I was little," Laney said. "I thought you would like it too."

Nothing.

"Well . . . you can get used to it later. What do you say we have sandwiches out by the pool?"

With a weary lift of her shoulders, Amy indicated she didn't care.

The sandwiches went untouched, and though Laney had convinced Amy to put on her new swimming suit, which proved to be a little tight, she couldn't get Amy to even stick her foot in the water. Finally giving up trying to pretend that they were getting along well, Laney pulled a chair up to face Amy. Amy seemed preoccupied with the hedges surrounding the yard.

"Amy, I know this is hard for you. Finding out I'm your mother and—"

"My mother died," the girl interrupted.

Laney paused. A warm breeze flitted through Amy's hair, and a strand reached across her lips. Laney reached out to push it back, but Amy recoiled from her touch. Laney's hand hovered in the air between them, and she told herself not to cry. Amy wasn't trying to hurt her. She was just trying to protect herself the best way she knew how. Controlling the ache of tears behind her eyes, Laney tried again. "I know how you feel. Believe it or not, I do. I lost my mom when I was nine. And things were never the same after that."

She got no reaction, but she went on. "Amy, I'm not trying to take the place of your mother or your father. It's just that I love you, too, and I want to know you. I want to be your friend."

"What time is it?" Amy asked coldly.

Failure, Laney thought. She was failing at the only thing that was important to her. Laney made herself breathe. "It's about four-thirty. Why?"

"I wish my daddy was here."

Laney accepted the child's verbal blow without letting the pain show on her face. "He isn't coming until six. But we could go ahead and start supper. I was going to make hamburgers and French fries. If you want, you can make the patties."

"No, thank you," Amy whispered.

A lump the size of her heart rose in Laney's throat, not to be swallowed down. "All right." She cleared her throat, but her voice still vibrated. "Let's go inside, then, and you can change back into your clothes and watch TV while I cook. I've been taping *Sesame Street* for the last few days. We could put the tape in."

"I'm too big for *Sesame Street,*" Amy said indignantly.

The last remnants of Laney's confidence dissolved. "We'll find something else, then."

Quietly she led Amy back into the house and flipped around for something on the television. When she drew no response from Amy, she withdrew to the kitchen.

She collapsed against the refrigerator as tears rolled down her cheeks. It's wrong, she thought miserably. All wrong. She had ruined everything! Laney ground her fist against her mouth to muffle her sobs. It wasn't working. Amy hated her. What was she going to do?

Methodically, she started to make the patties, pounding them into circles. She didn't even know if Amy *liked* hamburgers. When she'd planned it she'd been certain that every child liked them. But Amy's reaction had been so . . . indifferent.

Slapping a patty onto the wax paper, she wiped at her tears with the back of her hand. Amy's reaction to *everything* had been that way. Especially to her. Laney knew they couldn't go on this way. But today Amy was stronger than she was.

She had originally intended to cook the hamburgers on the grill, but that was when she'd planned for Amy to be enjoying herself in the pool. Fool of fools, she had even had visions of the three of them tossing a Frisbee while the smell of grilled burgers wafted across the yard. Now she set out a frying pan and dropped the patties in. When they and the French fries were under control, she went back to the den.

Amy was wiping her eyes, as if her tears were a weakness she needed desperately to hide. With a tiny sniffle, she turned her face away from Laney.

It was no use, Laney told herself. All the child wanted was to go home. Maybe sending her home would finally mean doing something right. Maybe they could try again tomorrow.

Stooping down in front of her, Laney set her hands on her daughter's knees. "Amy, I'm not going to make you stay here tonight if you don't want to. When your dad comes, you can go home with him if you want."

Amy wiped her eyes with the heels of her hand. "OK," she whispered.

OK, Laney thought. The least hostile word Amy had uttered all day. She had finally given Amy something she wanted.

Pulling herself together, she went back to the kitchen. The fries were popping, the burgers were sizzling, but Laney only stared at them. There was no need to slice tomatoes, wash lettuce, or chop onions. She had the dismal feeling that none of it would be eaten.

The doorbell rang, and she looked at her watch. It was a quarter to six, but she knew it was Wes, who had probably counted the minutes until he could see his daughter and make sure she was all right. If only she could open the door and let him see Amy giggling and playing, dragging him to her room to show him how beautiful it was, coaxing him into taking a swim. Instead, she would have to let him see that he'd been right all along.

Before Laney made it to the door, Amy had let her father in and had thrown her arms around his neck. She was clinging to him as if she couldn't bear the thought of him letting her go. His eyes met Laney's with alarm at the desperate embrace, but she had no reassurance to offer him.

"Daddy, can we go home?"

"Well, honey—"

"It's OK," Laney cut in, her lips trembling. "I told her that she could leave when you got here. She hasn't eaten all day, and she's hardly said anything . . ." Her voice trailed off, and she turned her face away. "I have supper ready, but if she doesn't want to—"

"I want to go home," Amy whispered.

Wes gave Laney a look that was half apology, half thanks. "She didn't sleep very well last night," he offered.

"None of us did," Laney said.

"No." Wes noted the red rims of Laney's eyes for the first time. He had been trying to see her as some shrew who manipulated life to make it suit her. What he saw now was a broken woman trying desperately to hold herself together until he left, the way he had done for her this morning. Love was a miserable thing, he thought suddenly. Their love for a child was destroying them, little by little. And it was destroying Amy.

Laney handed him Amy's overnight case, and tears brimmed in her eyes. "We'll try again, maybe tomorrow, huh, Amy?" she asked in a quivering voice.

Amy just buried her face in her father's neck.

Wes backed out of the doorway. "We'll talk after I get her settled down," he promised. "I'll call and we'll talk." *There has to be a better way,* his eyes said.

"I'll be here," she managed to say.

And as she watched him carry Amy to the car, she thought how ironic her last remark had been. Where else on earth would she go? She had no one except that little girl who had shattered her dreams in one day.

But as devastated as she was, Laney was still determined to make things work out. She was not going to say good-bye to her daughter again.

How were they all going to get through this? Wes asked himself later that night. Amy had cried her heart out all the way home, and she had collapsed in exhaustion before she'd even had a chance to eat.

It was just like a year ago when Patrice had died. He had been beside himself with his own grief, and yet his worry for Amy had forced him to keep it all in check. Why couldn't he keep her from hurting? Why couldn't he shelter her from more pain? What kind of father was he?

And what kind of woman was Laney? Couldn't she see what this was doing to Amy? How could she honestly suggest that they try again the next day?

He had promised to call. But what in the world would he say? Tomorrow was too soon. Next year was too soon. Never was too soon.

He sat on the couch and leaned his throbbing head back. The moment his eyes closed he was haunted with the image of a beautiful young woman with hair the color of raven's wings and hurting black eyes that begged for a chance. Life had been rough on her. But it had been rough on him too.

There were two kinds of people in this world, he had decided when Patrice first learned about her cancer. The ones who pranced through with hangnails and shallow dreams and the ones, like him, who dragged themselves through—praying for endurance, while sometimes wishing that they weren't strong enough to endure. Maybe then God would stop testing his faith.

What could he do? Run away? That in itself was a form of survival. But if he did that, uprooted Amy from the only home she'd ever known, wasn't he, in effect, doing the same thing that he had cursed Laney for? Wouldn't he be acting selfishly, cruelly? Wouldn't it instill a further sense of insecurity in his daughter?

And what would it do to Laney?

"I don't care what it does to her," he mumbled aloud. She was his last consideration. And yet . . .

The doorbell rang, and Wes looked at the front door grudgingly. So she couldn't wait for the phone call, he thought. She had to badger him some more in person.

His temper rose like mercury in a thermometer. Maybe it was time he spelled it out to her once and for all, he thought. Maybe he should explain exactly how she was destroying his and his daughter's lives. Maybe he could convince her that forcing Amy to acknowledge her could be psychologically devastating.

He opened the door, leaned against it, and stared down coldly at the woman who was ruining his life. But the fear shimmering in her eyes was the last offensive he expected, and the sad way she slumped against the casing pulled at every instinct to comfort that he possessed. That instinct made him angry, more at himself than at her. Silently, he stepped back from the door and let her in.

Laney had cried for hours after they left, realizing the hopelessness of what she was trying to do. When she had finally wept to the point of being physically ill, she had taken a shower and tried to calm herself down. She was not going to give up her daughter again. Maybe the plan they had worked out wasn't the best way. But there had to be other ways. And she was going to figure them out.

It had finally come to her, miraculously renewing that fragile bubble of hope that should have deflated long ago. She had dressed carefully, set ice cubes on her eyes to make the swelling go down, and applied her makeup. And then she had gone to see Wes.

He stood staring at her in the tiny foyer, his tired, angry eyes boring into her, telling her without words that she was the last person who was welcome in this house.

"I told you I'd call you," he said, abandoning the door and heading for the kitchen.

"I wanted to talk to you in person," she replied, following behind him. "Where's Amy?"

"In bed," he said. "She cried herself to sleep." He got a sponge and wiped the counters that were sticky from the dinner that had gone uneaten, then stared down at it with the slumped disillusionment of a man whose world teetered on the edge of a cliff.

"I'm not surprised," Laney said. "She was miserable."

He gave a mirthless laugh at her admission.

"What did you expect?" he asked, propping a shoulder against the wall as he watched her. "Did you think she'd just bubble over with joy that she was going to be living in two different places, one with a woman who popped into her life only a few months ago? A woman who used her money to make the court system disrupt her life?"

Laney tried to shield herself against the blows. "I don't know what I expected."

"I'll tell you what you expected." His voice was gravelly, its control only accenting the emotion that lurked beneath the surface. "You expected me to be such a lousy father that Amy would jump at the chance to have some real parenting for a change."

"I didn't think that," she said, finally aware that Wes was probably much more capable than she was.

He sighed and tossed the damp rag on the counter. "You told me a few weeks ago that your father wasn't equipped to raise a little girl. You thought I was—no, you thought all men were just like your father, that we couldn't feel and love and hurt. You thought a little girl couldn't really be happy being raised by a man because you were so miserable as a child. That's the whole reason for the lawsuit."

Laney swallowed back a new well of tears. "Wes, that's not true."

His eyes were brightening with his angry indictments, and he straightened and stepped tauntingly closer. "And since you were so miserable, you came back here determined to force everyone to make it up to you. You thought you could do it by taking Amy and manipulating her to be with you, so you could change things and make them right. You thought—"

"I thought wrong!" she exclaimed in a stage whisper. Her body wavered with the strength of her defenses, and she brought her glistening eyes to Wes's. "I was wrong. It can't really work that way."

For the first time since she'd walked in, Wes's mind went blank. For the love of God, he hadn't expected her to *admit* it. Was she giving up and going on her way, just like that? "You admit it?"

"Yes," she replied, closing her eyes against the tears. "I admit it. I admit it."

The defeated way she uttered the words reminded him of a wounded child cowering and pleading not to be hurt anymore. Suddenly he felt very small.

He stood looking down at her pained face, damming the surge of sympathy that rose inside him.

"Then . . . you don't plan to see her anymore?" he ventured. "You're giving up on this?"

Her chin came up, and she shook her head. "No, Wes. I'm not giving up. But I need your help."

"*My* help?" he asked, astounded.

81

"Yes," she said. "I need some ideas. Some support. You know Amy better than I do. What will make her open up? What will get through to her?"

He sank down onto the couch with a dry, mirthless laugh and stared incredulously at her. "You're kidding. You're really asking me to help you take her away from me?"

"That's not what I'm doing! I'm her mother, Wes, and the court said that we had a right to get to know each other. I'm asking you to make it easier for *her!* Have I asked for anything unreasonable? All I want is to keep her while you're at work, instead of some baby-sitter who doesn't have any stake in this. I want to take her shopping and fix her hair and teach her to cook . . . I want to give her the things that Patrice can't give her anymore. All I'm asking is for you, as her father, to help."

"She doesn't want to be with you, Laney. I can't force her to want that."

"She liked me before she knew who I was," Laney pointed out. "It's not me she hates. It's that feeling that I'm going to take her away from you. Maybe if you came, too, when I have her for the weekend, she wouldn't feel like we were enemies. She'd feel more secure."

He couldn't believe what he was hearing. "You're out of your mind. You take me to court and force me to share my daughter with you, and then you ask me to come along and give you moral support while you play mom with her?"

"Don't you see, Wes? She feels disloyal to Patrice and to you if she likes me. You have to make her understand that it's not a betrayal. I'm *adding* something to her life, not taking it away. If you could just pretend you didn't hate me . . ."

"I don't hate you."

"Of course you do." She wiped at the tears on her face. "Maybe I would hate me, too, if I were in your shoes. But that's because you don't understand. If I thought for a minute that Amy would be better off without me, I'd leave town and never come back. But in my heart I know all that I can give her, Wes."

Wes's eyes settled on a spot on the wall as he tried not to feel the truth in what she was saying. She wasn't demanding to rip Amy out of her home, uproot her, and force her to get used to the joint custody arrangement. She really was thinking of the child. Maybe more than he was.

"If I say no?"

She looked even more crushed than before. "Then . . . then it only hurts Amy. Her confusion, her worry . . . it won't be relieved. She'll stay in pain."

"And you think that our playing this as a team will end her pain?"

"I think it'll help."

He set his elbows on his knees and stared down at the floor between his feet. "I don't want to spend time with you, Laney. I don't want to pretend we're pals. I don't want my daughter to like you."

"I know you don't," she whispered. "But will you do it anyway? You might find out that I'm not the monster you think I am."

He looked up at her again and thought that he had never considered her a monster. She was pretty and sad and even when he was most angry with her, he'd never been able to work up enough contempt against her to hate her. A big part of him understood why she was doing what she was doing. It just didn't make it easier.

"All right," he said finally. "Tomorrow. We'll hang out like we're great friends, and I'll put on an Oscar-winning performance. But I have one condition."

"What?"

"I want to take her to church first."

She hesitated for a moment. "Why church?"

"Because I want my daughter in church on Sundays."

The idea seemed to disturb her. "Well, I don't think I would feel comfortable going to your church. Your friends all probably know about the lawsuit. The idea of sitting there with people judging me doesn't really appeal to me at all."

"Then I'll take her alone, and we'll come to your house afterward."

"It's not that I don't want to go, you understand. I mean, I don't have anything against church. I haven't been in years . . . My father didn't worship anything that didn't first worship him. But I'm glad you take Amy. The values they learn there are good. I realize that."

"It's not about values to us. It's about worship. Amy doesn't like to miss it."

"OK, then," she said. "I'll cook lunch. You can come over afterward. We can swim, go to the park, maybe take in a movie . . ."

"All in one afternoon?" he asked.

She swallowed. "I have a lot of catching up to do, Wes."

He followed her to the door and watched as she pulled out of his driveway. Tomorrow they would be pals, he thought. Or they would pretend to. Was it the right thing, or was he just selling out?

Lord, I don't want to be her friend.

But that wasn't an option, he realized. He had to be her friend. Amy needed him to. And maybe, deep in his heart, he needed it as well.

CHAPTER EIGHT

Normally, being around a beautiful woman in a swimsuit put Wes in a great mood. But he didn't want to notice Laney, so he kept his eyes off her for most of the afternoon. And that resulted in what seemed like brooding. Which fed Amy's brooding.

Laney tried to engage them in a game of Marco Polo, but Amy refused to play. Then she strung up a volleyball net in the pool, but Amy wasn't interested. Quickly, she took it back down.

When the child got out of the pool and dried off, Laney swam over to Wes as he sat on the edge of the pool, making every effort to focus on something other than the woman who attracted him more than he dared admit.

"You're not trying very hard," Laney accused in a whisper.

She had no idea how hard he was trying, he thought. "Laney, I'm not sure what you want me to do."

"Pretend to have fun," she said. "Pretend you like me, at least a little. Play, splash around, flirt, for heaven's sake. Just do something! Amy's not ever going to relax as long as all this tension is between us."

He finally allowed himself to look at her. It wasn't that her swimsuit was inappropriate. It actually bordered on prudish. But there was something about her today . . . "Flirt?" he asked. "You're crazy."

"Why? I'm just asking you to be playful, like you were at the playground with her. Laugh a little. Pick her up and throw her around. Dunk me. Help me get something going here."

Sighing as if it took every bit of effort he had, he slid into the water and forced a smile on his face. Halfheartedly he splashed her.

Halfheartedly, she splashed him back.

He glanced at Amy and saw that they had her rapt attention. He glanced back at Laney.

Wes didn't know what came over him, but suddenly he felt injected with a mischievousness that had to be played out. He turned away from Laney, dove underwater, and swam away from her. Then doing a quick U-turn, he headed back.

She had turned away and was heading for the ladder.

Wes rammed her legs from behind, flipping her up. She screamed and went under and came up sputtering, determined to get even.

She grabbed his head, pushed him under, but he caught hold of a foot and dragged her across the pool. "Bull-headed woman. Thinks she can push me under!" He lifted her and threw her several feet in front of him as she screamed and struggled.

Amy was at the side, smiling grudgingly.

Laney got her bearings and swam toward him, grinning, intent on payback. "This is war, Grayson."

"Oh, yeah?" he asked, diving under and grabbing her feet again before she could reach him. She was laughing when he came up, and he shouted, "What was that you said it was? War?"

"Do me, Daddy!" Amy shouted.

Wes swam to the ladder and quickly got out. "Do you?" he asked Amy. "Is that what you said?"

She screamed with glee as he picked her up and tossed her in, then dove in behind her. When she came up, he laughed wickedly. "I can take both of you women."

"Let's get him, Amy!" Laney shouted.

Together, they swam toward him, and Wes allowed them each to grab a foot and flip him over.

When he came up, they were both rolling in laughter. It was a small step, seeing them laugh together, he thought. A step he had given to Laney though his heart had advised him not to.

He didn't know whether it had been the right thing or not, but he did know that it was good to see his little girl laughing and playing again. Acting indignant, he went after them both and shoved their heads underwater.

The mock war in the pool loosened Amy up considerably, giving Laney hope. When they were all exhausted from the fierce water wrestling, they changed clothes and ordered a pizza. But Amy was asleep on the couch with her head in her father's lap before the pizza even arrived.

"She must have been tired," Laney said, smiling as she gazed down at the sleeping child. "Do you want me to get her a blanket?"

"No, I think she's warm enough," he said softly. He looked up at Laney. Her hair was still damp and stringing around her shoulders, and she didn't have an ounce of makeup on. But she was still beautiful. It was something about her he almost dreaded, for it made it more difficult to remember reality. He wished she wasn't Amy's mother. If she had just been a beautiful woman he had met somewhere, if he could have asked her out to dinner, spent time with her, gotten to know her, things would be so much different.

She got down on her knees in front of them and stroked Amy's hair back from her face, gazing at her with a tenderness that he'd seen so often in Patrice's eyes. She did love Amy; he had no doubt about that.

So why did he resist her so? he asked himself. Wasn't the fact that she was a built-in part of their lives more of a reason for him to get to know her?

No, he told himself. It was a reason to stay away, to keep his feelings harnessed, to continue holding his contempt for her like a shield over his chest. She was the biggest threat in his life.

She got back to her feet and sat down on the couch next to him. "I really appreciate what you did today," she said. "It was a dream come true. Maybe tomorrow when I pick her up from school, she won't shut me out."

He had forgotten about tomorrow. "She was OK today because I was here, Laney. But tomorrow, it'll just be you and her again. Maybe it's too soon."

"I have to try," Laney said. "But what if I cook you supper? She could help, and knowing that you're coming, she might relax more."

He looked at her, the tension on his face deepening his tired lines. "I can cook her supper. You didn't say anything about that when you asked to keep her after school."

Her face fell at the tone in his voice. "Well, no, but she has to eat. So do you. And I just thought—"

"She should probably eat at home," he said.

She compressed her lips and looked down at the sleeping child. For a moment, there was silence between them, and finally she asked, "What if I cook you a casserole or something and you can take it home?"

He looked up at her. What was she trying to do? Win his heart through his stomach? Or did she harbor some fantasy of being responsible for both of them, as if he were as much her family as Amy was?

But just as suddenly as he'd entertained those thoughts, he realized he could be wrong. She had no family. And as far as he could tell, no friends. Not here, anyway. Maybe she was just desperately lonely.

Wes understood loneliness.

Sighing, he finally said, "Look, if you really want to cook, I guess there's no harm. I'll come over after work and eat with you, but then I'm taking Amy home."

"Fine," Laney said, her eyes brightening again. "I'll see that she gets all her homework done, so you don't have to worry about it tomorrow night. And I'll take her to the park, so she can play with her friends."

He nodded. She was trying so hard that it was growing more and more difficult to see her as a negative in Amy's life . . . or his, either, for that matter. But he had to, he thought. He couldn't let himself see her as anything else.

"I think she's out for the night," he said. "I'd better take her home."

Laney's eyes betrayed her disappointment, but she got up and began gathering the clothes Amy had changed from after church, the little stockings and the Sunday shoes. Wes lifted her and let her head rest on his shoulder.

Laney followed him out to the truck and fastened the child's seat belt around her hips, then helped her to lie down in her father's lap as he cranked the engine.

"I'll see you tomorrow," she said quietly.

"Yeah." He knew he should thank her for the afternoon, but something stopped him. She closed the door and stepped back, and he pulled out of the driveway.

When he glanced in his rearview mirror, she was still standing in the yard, watching with a poignant expression as they drove out of sight.

Wes had just finished the bid for the buildings at the new amusement park going up across town and was gathering his things to go pick Amy up at Laney's when Sherry burst into his office, waving a letter in her hand. "It's happened! Oh, Wes, this is from the bank!"

He snatched the letter out of her hand and scanned the contents. The bank was foreclosing on his house, and he had two weeks to get out.

For a moment, he just stared at it, too numb to react. "This can't be happening. They're not taking my house."

"Read on! They're also taking this building, the computer, all the equipment, everything anybody owes you . . ."

He flung the letter down and kicked his desk. "I'm finished with the bid for the amusement park! If we get this job, I can pay off the debts, and I've got a great chance. I've known Andi Sherman for years, and she'll be the one to decide. I've got to hold them off!"

"But, Wes, it could be weeks before they decide who gets the contract. You haven't got time!"

He grabbed the telephone and dialed the number for his lawyer. "This is Wes Grayson. I need to speak to Bert Hampton. It's urgent."

"I'm sorry," his secretary said. "He's left for the day."

Wes checked his watch. He was supposed to be at Laney's already. He'd promised Amy this morning when he'd explained why she had to go back today.

"Is he at home?"

"I think so."

Without thanking her, Wes hung up, then searched his Rolodex for the man's home number. Finally he found it, dialed, and waited.

"Hello?"

"Bert, this is Wes Grayson. You've got to help me, man."

"What's going on?"

"They're giving me two weeks to get out of my house. They're taking everything."

"All right, Wes. Meet me at my office in fifteen minutes. I'll head back over."

Wes hung up and grabbed the letter off the floor. Too preoccupied to say good-bye to his sister, he hurried out the door.

Where's my daddy?" Amy asked, sitting at the front window of the house, where she had been for the past hour. "He said he'd be here at five-thirty."

"He's just a little late," Laney said. "He'll be here. Why don't we go ahead and eat, and then we can warm up a plate for him when he gets here?"

"No," Amy said. "I'm not hungry."

From the window, the child could see the end of the street and every car that turned into the neighborhood. She watched and waited, tense and expectant.

"Why don't I get us some construction paper or something and we can make something while we wait? Would you like that?"

"No."

Laney sat down next to her, trying to hide her disappointment. The afternoon hadn't gone as well as she'd hoped, but it had been tolerable. Though Amy had ignored her most of the time, she had managed to have fun at the park, and she had grudgingly allowed Laney to help her with her homework. She hadn't been interested in helping her cook but had sat quietly on the couch watching *The Little Mermaid* as Laney worked in the kitchen.

Now she could see the distress rising in the little girl's face as she waited for her father. Laney had tried to call his office, but there had been no answer. She was sure he'd be here soon, and then she hoped the child would relax again, like she had in the pool yesterday. If she could just get Amy away from this window.

"Amy, I haven't put the icing on the cake I made for dessert yet. Do you want to do it?"

"No."

"Why not?"

"Because."

"Honey, your daddy must have had something come up. He knows you're fine here with me, so he isn't worried. He'll come when he can."

A big tear dropped onto Amy's cheek.

Laney caught her breath and knelt in front of her. "Honey, what's the matter?"

Her bottom lip puckered out, and her face began to redden.

Laney pushed back the child's hair and wiped the tears from her cheeks. "Please, Amy. Tell me what's wrong."

"He's not coming, is he?" Amy asked in a squeak. "He's leaving me here with you. He was just tricking me when he said he would come."

"Oh, honey, no!" Laney insisted. "He meant it. He'll be here. I promise you. Daddy would never say he was coming to get you if he didn't mean it."

"Yes, he would!" Amy cried. "Mommy did."

Laney's heart shattered, and she reached out for the child, but Amy swirled off her chair and backed away. "Sweetheart, Mommy didn't lie to you."

"Yes, she did! She went to the hospital, and she promised me she was coming back home! But she never did! She tricked me, just like Daddy!"

Laney covered her mouth with her hand. "Amy, Mommy was real sick. She wanted to come home more than anything in the whole world. But she couldn't. She didn't break her promise to you. She just never got the chance to keep it."

She reached for Amy again, but the child recoiled. "Honey, listen to me—"

It was then that she heard the muffled sound of an engine pulling into the driveway, and she looked through the window. "There he is!" she shouted victoriously. "See? Your daddy came. Just like he said he would!"

Amy caught her breath and bolted for the front door. She was halfway across the yard before Wes was out of the truck.

He picked her up and she clung to him, weeping with her face buried in his neck. He fixed angry, accusing eyes on Laney as she approached him. "What did you do to her?"

Laney sucked in a breath. "Nothing! She got upset because you were late! She thought you weren't coming!"

He whispered into Amy's ear, trying to soothe her, then glanced back at Laney. "Look, I'm just gonna take her home. Neither one of us is up to doing dinner tonight. I'll pick her up a hamburger on the way home."

Laney nodded. "All right." She watched as he pried Amy off him and made her climb into the truck. "Wes, tomorrow will you explain to her that you might be late, but you're still coming?"

He cranked the engine before he answered her. "I can't believe you'd bring her out this upset and expect to do it all again tomorrow."

Laney was getting angry. "Wes, she wasn't upset until you were late! And I would think you'd at least offer some kind of explanation! To her, if not to me."

"Something came up," he said between tight lips. "I got here as soon as I could."

"Fine," she said, backing off.

He put the truck in reverse and gave her one last look as if he had something to say but couldn't say it. Finally, he backed out without a word.

Laney headed back into the house as fast as she could before he could see her crying again.

N ot long after they left, the phone rang. Laney cleared her throat and wiped the tears off her face before she picked up the receiver. "Hello?"

"Uh . . . this is Sherry Grayson . . . Wes's sister? Is he still there, by any chance?"

"No," she said, trying not to sound so forlorn. "He left about fifteen minutes ago."

"Oh. I was hoping to catch him to warn him before he went home."

Laney frowned. "Warn him of what?"

"Of the sign the bank posted on his house. I went by there to drop off some groceries I picked up for him, and I saw it. He isn't even out yet, and they've already set a date for the auction."

"What auction?"

"His house. Didn't he tell you?"

Laney got to her feet. "Are they foreclosing on his house?"

"Uh . . . well . . . look," she said, obviously rattled. "I'll just call him when he gets home. I'm sorry to bother you."

Laney hung up and stared disbelievingly down at the phone. Was that why Wes was late? Had he just learned that the bank was foreclosing on his house?

Slowly she sank down onto the couch, wishing she hadn't yelled back when he'd yelled at her. But he hadn't said a thing about foreclosure. Was he really being forced to leave his and Amy's home?

Darkness began to descend, but Laney didn't bother to turn on any lights. Instead, she sat alone on her couch, staring into the dusk and trying to imagine what it would do to Amy to lose her home now, on top of all the stress that Laney had brought into the little girl's life.

She thought of Amy's tears today, how she'd been certain that Wes wasn't coming back, that he'd "tricked" her, that he, like her mother, was fading out of her life.

So much instability, she thought. So much uncertainty.

This was even worse than when Laney was a child. At least her father hadn't had money problems. She had been able to stay in the home she'd shared with her mother. She wondered how her life would have been if there had been another mother figure somewhere, someone who wanted to love her and take care of her. Would she have welcomed it or shunned it? Would it have helped her through her grief or heightened it?

She opened the back door and walked back to the pool. Standing on the edge, she thought of Sunday afternoon when they'd played together like a family in the water, pretending that no one was missing, no one was added, nothing was broken, nothing was lost . . . She had clung to that fantasy ever since, not for herself as much as for Amy. She couldn't help remembering how Amy had acted the first day they met, before she saw Laney as a threat. She had needed a woman in her life—in her home. And she had chosen to warm up to Laney.

It could be that way again, if some of the stress was relieved and some of the uncertainty were taken away. She could win Amy over if she could only get past some of the obstacles in her way.

It didn't matter what it cost Laney. Somehow she had to find a way to bring stability instead of uncertainty back into Amy's life.

A vague thought dawned on her, a thought that would offer Wes some relief and perhaps serve as a peace offering between them. She could loan him the money he needed to keep his house.

But that would only solve one of the problems, she thought. Not all of them. It would relieve his immediate stress, but it still wouldn't bring Amy family security or give rest to her frightened mind. And it wouldn't help her to accept Laney.

Laney wanted to be a mother, not just a creditor.

But there might be another way.

As a better idea took root in her heart, she began to see the light of hope. Maybe it would work. Maybe it could solve everything.

Quickly, she grabbed her purse and dug for her car keys. She had to see Wes right away.

Sherry showed up around eight with all the sympathy a sister could give, and knowing that Wes was too preoccupied and upset to function normally, she supervised Amy's bath and put her to bed. After she had read Amy a story that put her to sleep, she looked for Wes.

He wasn't in the den, so she went to the doorway of his bedroom and peeked in. Wes sat on the side of his bed, staring down at the portrait of Patrice in his hand.

"Want to talk?" Sherry asked him.

He twisted his mouth and shrugged. "I was just thinking what a failure I am. She trusted me to hold things together. I've lost partial custody of Amy, and I can't even hold onto my house. I can't even make a living."

"Wes, none of this is your fault. You didn't ask Laney Fields to come into your life. And nobody can blame you for all of the bills from Patrice's cancer. What were you gonna do? Turn down medical treatment for her because you couldn't afford it?"

"It's gonna kill Amy, leaving this house."

"You can stay with me until you get an apartment or find something to rent."

"First I have to find a job."

"But maybe you'll get the contract for the park. Maybe it'll happen in time . . ."

Wes shook his head. "No. They won't make a decision on that for three weeks. By then, the bank will have everything I own. Let's face it. I'm finished."

"You can't get an extension?"

"No," he said. "This *was* an extension. I've been putting them off for months."

She sat down on the bed next to him and hugged him. "I'm so sorry, Wes. I wish there was something I could do."

"You did a lot. Working for me all these weeks with no pay . . ." He swallowed and looked down at the picture again. "I guess I'll tell Amy tomorrow. We'll have to start moving out this weekend. Maybe I could hire on with one of my subcontractors and get him to advance me a deposit on an apartment. I just hate to do it all so fast. It doesn't give her any time to get used to it . . ."

He broke into tears and covered his face, and Sherry didn't know what to do for him.

The doorbell rang, and he drew in a deep breath.

"Who could that be?" Sherry asked.

"Maybe the bank, coming to take all the furniture," he said. "Bloodsuckers . . ."

Sherry got up. "I'll get it."

He went to the bathroom and leaned over the sink to splash water on his face. Blotting his face with a towel, he looked into the mirror. He had aged ten years in the last one, he thought. He had put up a terrible fight to stay above water, but he had lost.

He could accept all of it stoically, he thought, if it weren't for Amy.

Sherry came back into the bedroom. "Wes, it's Laney Fields."

He came out, frowning. "What does she want?"

"Well, uh . . . she sort of heard about what was going on . . ."

"How?"

Sherry winced. "I called you over there earlier, and I sort of . . . mentioned it before I realized she didn't already know."

"Oh, great," he said. "She's probably come to chastise me for not providing for my child. Thanks a lot, Sherry."

"I'm sorry, Wes. Look, I'm going to go home now, but if you need anything, just call. Any time of the night. I mean it, OK?" She shot him a bolstering look, then turned and headed for the back door.

He watched her go, his eyes dull. He didn't want to see Laney. Not now. But as always, she hadn't given him a choice in the matter.

Laney was waiting in the den. The moment she saw him, she asked, "Wes, why didn't you tell me about the foreclosure?"

He threw up his hands. "I'm sorry. I must have missed the part where the judge told me I had to keep you informed about every event in my life."

"Not every one," she said, "but where you'll live, at least. Have you told Amy?"

"No, I haven't told Amy," he said impatiently. "I'm still trying to sort it all out myself."

"Well . . . when do you have to move?"

"Two weeks," he said. "We'll probably go ahead and get out this weekend."

"Poor Amy," she said, sinking down on the couch. "It's gonna be such a shock to her."

"She's getting used to shocks," he said. "You never cared about them before."

"She's getting used to me," Laney said. "When you were late tonight, it was just a setback. She got scared. Wes, did she tell you what she was afraid of?"

He shook his head and ran a hand through his hair, leaving it tousled. "No. We didn't really talk about it much."

"She said that she thought you'd tricked her like her mommy did."

"What?"

"Wes, she's terrified of losing you. She said that her mother promised to come back, and she didn't, and now she's sure that one day you won't either."

"She told you that?"

"Yes. She was very upset. It was . . . one of the worst things I've ever seen. It reminded me of my childhood so much . . ." Her lips began to quiver. She was trembling, trying to go on. Finally she looked up. "Amy needs you," she said. "She's afraid, I think, that if she gets comfortable with me, she'll lose you altogether. I think in her seven-year-old head she may even think we're trying to prepare her for a time when you'll drop out of her life."

Knocking a newspaper off of a chair, Wes wilted into it. His eyes grew luminous. Maybe she did understand after all. "No argument so far."

"On the other hand, the way she warmed up to me before she knew I was her mother told me that she very much wanted a woman in her life. She's hungry for a mother, not because of anything that you *can't* provide, but because of what a woman *can*."

Wes frowned. She was leading up to something. He could feel it.

"And I've been thinking about that an awful lot lately. And then tonight when I heard about the foreclosure . . . I couldn't help thinking what could solve everything."

"What?" he asked, dumbfounded that she would be presumptuous enough to think that anything regarding her would solve his problems.

"Separately," she went on cautiously, "we can't change things for the better. Only for the worse. But together—"

"What are you saying?" Not what he thought. Surely not that.

Laney took a deep breath and pushed back a strand of hair. "I'm saying that—I mean, I'm suggesting that in order to give her what she needs and maybe make things easier on ourselves, that maybe we should . . ." Her voice trailed off, too weak to go on.

"Should what?" he asked impatiently.

"Should . . . get married. For Amy's sake."

A breathless moment followed as Wes erupted out of his chair. "Are you nuts? You've got to be out of your mind! For Amy's sake?"

he asked, astounded. "Have you honestly convinced yourself that you'd be doing this for Amy's sake?"

"Why else would I do it?"

"For your sake, maybe? Instant child, instant husband, instant home?" The astonishment drained from his voice, and something almost violent replaced it. "Since there happens to be an opening in this family, maybe you thought you could slip right in and fill it?"

She wouldn't let herself get angry. Her voice was a carefully controlled monotone. "No. I've thought this out. It would benefit all of us. Even you. Especially where money is concerned."

"I don't have any money."

"Obviously. But I do." She steadied her breathing. It was time to lay all her cards on the table. Everything was at stake. "I have lots of it, and you need it. You can hold onto your pride and lose your home, or you can do what I'm suggesting and save everything."

His mouth opened with disbelief. "So let me get this straight. If I marry you, you'll pay me off?"

"No," she said. "I'm saying that if you marry me, everything I have will be yours. My father's inheritance, my house, everything. None of it means anything to me. Amy's the only thing that matters."

"My daughter and I are not for sale!"

"I'm not trying to buy you," she retorted. "It's Amy's money too. She was his granddaughter. She deserves it. He disrupted our lives, ruined mine, and he owed me, just like he owed her. If it's Amy's money, why should it bother you to let her help pay her mother's hospital bills and help her father's company get back on its feet?"

"Because I don't like what goes with it," he said.

She steeled herself against yet another blatant rejection. "I'll help you." Her voice shook with the words. Good heavens, was she pleading now? She tried to mask the desperation in her voice. "I'll be there all day, taking care of Amy in her own home, keeping the house clean, and cooking meals. You won't feel so divided. And when you get home, you can relax. I can be a good mother and a good wife. Amy will have two parents at the same time, and she'll be happier. You must see that."

When Wes turned back to her, tears were glistening in his eyes. "I don't want to get married again," he whispered. "Never."

"Not even for Amy?"

He glared at her for a hateful moment, as if she had trumped his ace. "You want to be my wife?" he asked sarcastically. "When you don't even have a clue what a wife is?"

"I can learn," she whispered. "And I'll stay out of your way. If we got married, I wouldn't try to take Patrice's place. I wouldn't expect love or even respect. I wouldn't expect anything. I just want to be with my baby. We could try to be friends, try to like each other."

He turned his back to her and searched his mind and heart for some order, some answers. What would it be like to have her in his home every day? How would it feel, sharing Amy with her, sharing the responsibility, the love? How would it feel to share his and Patrice's home with a woman he hardly knew?

He couldn't. He shook his head, unable to consider it anymore. "It's blackmail," he said. "If you really cared about what losing everything is going to do to Amy, then you'd offer me a loan, not marriage!"

"I've thought of that," she said. "But I don't want to loan it to you, Wes. I want to give it to you. I want to be a mother, not a banker. Money alone isn't what Amy needs. If you marry me, you'll have access to my whole inheritance. I wouldn't hold any of it back."

Wes turned back to her. She was still begging, still willing to sacrifice. "It can't work, Laney," he said too loudly. "Marriage is a sacred institution to me. God didn't create it to be like that. Besides, it would make Amy's home life as strained as it is when she's with you." Not to mention his own life, he thought.

"Just for a while," she pleaded. "If she thought it was a real marriage, that we really loved each other the way a husband and wife do, she might accept it. She wouldn't see me as the enemy trying to invade her life. The stress is going to get a lot worse if you lose your house, Wes."

He set his hands on his hips and stared at her. Did she think he hadn't considered that?

"Even if you say no, you aren't going to get rid of me," she promised him. "I'm here to stay. I'm trying to find alternatives, but the court gave me joint custody, and I intend to use it."

"You mean you'd put her through what she went through today? Sobbing and remembering her mother, thinking her father isn't going to come home? You'd do that again?"

"I wouldn't want to!" Laney said. "But I'm convinced she needs me. And I need her."

Wes ruffled his hair and looked at the ceiling, a despondent, futile look coloring his twisted features. "I can't do it. I can't make a mockery of marriage after Patrice."

She felt herself losing the battle and knew this loss might cost her the war. "Please, Wes," she said, touching his back. "Don't think of it that way. I wouldn't push you or expect anything. It wouldn't be like a real marriage, except to Amy. You and I would know differently. And when she grows up—"

"What about you?" he asked suddenly, turning back to her. "You'd be destroying any chance you have for finding someone else. A *real* husband. You'd be locking yourself into a false life and giving up a real one."

"And so would you."

His shrug was hopeless. "I've already had my life."

His words were dispassionate and final. Had he really laid his heart to rest with Patrice? "Then give me mine," she entreated. "It's an agreement, that's all. It can be broken."

"Just like that?"

"If it isn't working, I'll be the first to admit it."

When he turned away again she slid her hand up his back and closed it over his shoulder. "Please, Wes," she whispered in a strained voice. "You've never thanked me for giving you my daughter. She was the only thing in life that ever mattered to me. Please give me the chance to get her back. I promise I'll never take her from you."

Somehow her last words had more impact than all the others she'd prepared tonight. *I'll never take her from you.* It was a way to ensure that. He could never hope to see her give up and walk away. They had come much too far.

And Amy did need a mother. He closed his eyes and recalled the helpless feeling he'd had earlier when he hadn't known what to say to her, when he hadn't been able to comfort her. She had needed Patrice, but she had Laney instead.

"I'm a Christian," he whispered. "I believe in living my life a certain way. Church is an important part of our life, and so is our faith. I won't sacrifice my beliefs for you."

"I'm not asking you to," she said. "I . . . I've never been a church-goer, but I'll start. And I've never really believed in God, but I'll try. Please, just give me a chance, Wes. I promise I'll never compromise the things you've taught Amy. And I'll do my best to live by them."

"Living by them means that you don't enter into a temporary, frivolous marriage for the sake of convenience. If I get married again, it'll be for life. For better or for worse."

"Fine," she said. "No back door. I can accept that."

"I'm not offering it."

She sighed and struggled to find the right words. "Be reasonable, Wes. You're a businessman. This is a business arrangement. You wouldn't hesitate to hire a live-in nanny. Think of me as that. It's what's best for Amy."

"You just don't get it, do you?"

"Get what?"

"Marriage isn't a business arrangement *or* a game."

"And bankruptcy and joint custody are no picnic. I want more for my daughter. And I know you do, too."

He stared at her for a moment, the agony in his eyes still resisting defeat.

"It's blackmail," he said again, raking a hand through his hair.

"That's not fair," she said. "I'm not threatening you into this."

"Aren't you?"

She looked at the floor and shook her head dolefully. "Just think about it, Wes. With an open mind. Think about what's best for her. It's the only answer that makes any sense."

He fixed his eyes on her then, staring at her as moments ticked by. She was sure he was going to say yes. Sure that he knew it was the only way.

"I don't have to think about it," he said finally. "The answer is no."

CHAPTER NINE

The next morning, Wes sat alone in the small building that had housed his business for the last several years. He couldn't believe he was going to lose it. He glanced up at the plaque that he'd won three years ago, for "Builder of the Year." His business had been booming then, and he'd developed a reputation for reliable, honest, high-quality work.

Who would have believed it would come to this?

He heard a car pulling up on the gravel parking lot and through the window saw his lawyer. More bad news, he thought, bracing himself. What more could they take away?

He met Bert at the door and reached out to shake his hand. "How are you doing, Wes?" the tired-looking attorney asked.

"I'm OK," he said. "Still a little numb, but OK."

Bert pulled up a chair and sat down to face him. "I just wanted to let you know that I tried for another extension. They wouldn't give it."

"Yeah, well, you didn't think they would."

Bert looked down at his feet. "Man, I wish I had the money to loan you myself."

"It's a lot of money," Wes said.

Bert looked back up at him. "I feel like I've let you down a lot lately. First on the custody thing, and now this . . ."

Wes shook his head and got up. "It wasn't your fault, Bert. We're gonna be all right. I just haven't been able to tell Amy yet that we've got to move out. I keep putting it off."

"I don't blame you. She's been through enough lately." Bert paused and adjusted his glasses. "By the way, I was thinking this morning, and it occurred to me that you might want to keep this foreclosure from Laney Fields. Is there any way you can hide it? Make it look like you just willfully decided to move?"

"No, it's too late. She already knows."

Bert groaned.

"Why?"

Bert got up and slid his hands under his coat and into his pants pockets. "Well, I was just afraid she might take advantage of it. Try to take you back to court for full custody."

"Full custody?" The words knocked him back. "Why would she do that?"

"Well, she could say that you don't have a job or a home and convince the judge that the child is better off with her right now. I was just thinking it was better if you could avoid it."

Wes stood frozen for a moment, trying to think as Laney might think. Would Laney do that? No, he thought. She couldn't. "I don't think Laney would be that opportunistic," he said. "She does seem to care about Amy. She knows it would only hurt Amy to take her completely away."

"People can convince themselves of some crazy things, Wes. I'd look out, if I were you. Don't give her too much ammunition. How did she react to the foreclosure?"

Wes almost laughed. "Well, you wouldn't believe me if I told you."

"Try me."

The amusement left his eyes and faded into weariness. "She asked me to marry her."

"What?" The lawyer almost choked. "Marry her?"

"Yeah. She said she'd give me all the money I needed to bail me out of this. All I had to do was plug her into Patrice's place . . ." His voice trailed off as he saw that his lawyer wasn't amused anymore.

"And what did you say?"

"I told her no. In no uncertain terms."

Bert nodded. "I see."

"You see what?" Wes asked. "You don't think I ought to marry her!"

"No." Bert shook his head and stroked his chin. "No, of course not. I'm just wondering if this doesn't prove my point. What will she do if you don't? Do you think she'll take further action?"

"Well, I don't think so." He looked down at the floor, remembering the way she had pleaded with him. She was desperate; that was clear. And she had called his bluff and taken legal action before.

Bert's face reflected his grave concern as he studied Wes. "Wes, I know that marrying her must seem ludicrous to you. But if you say no, maybe you ought to do it gently. Don't make her mad."

"Bert, you sound like you're afraid of her."

"I'm afraid of the power she might have," Bert said. "Wes, if she does happen to take you back to court, chances are, you could lose Amy once and for all. I'd tread real lightly around Laney Fields if I were you."

Days later, as he waited for the time to pick Amy up from Laney's, at which time he would tell her that she was about to lose the home where all her mother's memories still lived, Wes sat on his bed, leaning back against the headboard.

Not for the first time since Laney suggested it, he wondered if marrying her could really be an option to keep him from having to break his child's heart.

It wasn't as if Laney were some hag or some terrible influence on his daughter. If he thought about it rationally, he might even see it as a blessing. It might even be what Patrice would have wanted.

After all, he had neither the time, money, nor inclination for single's bars or health clubs, and his church had very few single women. Where else did a single man go to meet women to find companionship? If he'd ordered her specifically, he couldn't have been offered a better blend of what he needed. Not just any mother for Amy. Her real mother. Not just any woman for himself. A woman he'd already found himself attracted to.

But what of love? And what of those bonds that had made his marriage with Patrice work? What of having things in common, things to share, things that made them enjoy each other's company?

He didn't know about any of those things with Laney because he'd never had the chance to find out. Theirs had been a relationship of enmity from the first day he'd laid eyes on her. And it hadn't gotten any better.

He opened his eyes and looked at the portrait of Patrice on his bedside table. Another wife, he thought, to fill the empty slot where only she had the right to be. He took the picture, frowning as he caressed the frame.

Swallowing the pain gathering in his throat, he pulled open the drawer and slipped the picture in. His breath grew thin, his heart constricted, and he stared at the open drawer. Closing it was a Herculean task he wasn't prepared for.

He lifted the photograph back out of the drawer and returned it to the table. "I still can't do it," he whispered brokenly. "I just can't." He rubbed his face wearily and lay down on the bed, staring at the serenely smiling woman in the photo. "I can't replace you."

His eyes misted, and he moved his blurred focus to the ceiling, searching for an answer. But no matter how he had searched over the past year, he couldn't escape the cold, dark loneliness that bordered on the unbearable, topped with scattered memories that he wanted desperately not to fade.

And how much more unbearable would that loneliness be with a woman he didn't love sharing his home and his daughter?

He pulled off the bed and went to Amy's room. Sitting on her bed, he picked up her small teddy bear and hugged it against his chest. She was so young, and she needed a mother. He still wasn't sure why God had allowed her to end up without one. Maybe this was God's way of working things out, he thought. Maybe he had sent Laney to them.

And maybe not.

He closed his eyes and tried to pray—for wisdom and discernment and the strength to follow God's will. But the prayer didn't come easily, and he recalled the days after Patrice's death when he had been so steeped in his own pain that he couldn't pray at all. He had relied then on the prayers of those who loved him and on God's faithfulness to carry him when he wasn't able to walk.

Maybe this was one of those times. Still, he knelt beside her bed and tried.

But as he did, his daughter's needs became the most important in his mind. Amy needed a mother, but she also needed stability. Laney was offering the chance to be a mother to her without disrupting her life. What difference did it make, really, if he felt bad about it? What difference did it make if it made him happy or not?

His daughter had lost her mother, and now she was losing her home. He was losing his income, and the security he had wanted so much to provide Amy was a thing of the past.

Laney had offered him the chance to change all that.

"Wes, if she does happen to take you back to court, chances are, you could lose Amy once and for all."

Bert was right. The threat was there, whether she had uttered it or not. She could convince herself that she was doing the best thing for Amy and remove Wes completely from his child's life. He'd be like a divorced father with alternate weekend visitation. It was something that he couldn't stand the thought of.

On the other hand, if he took her offer, he could keep Amy in her own home, his business wouldn't go under, and Laney, who had joint custody already anyway, would be able to mother Amy without taking her from him.

He dropped his head on the side of the bed and cried out to God to give him wisdom, but it seemed that his mind and heart were too full to allow room for the Holy Spirit. Defeated and hopeless, he found himself making a decision he had never believed he would make, but the only one he could justify. It was the least harmful decision for Amy. It was the safest one for them all.

Wondering if he was finally crossing the threshold of insanity, he got up, found his keys, and headed over to Laney's.

CHAPTER TEN

When Wes told Laney that he would agree to marry her, she seemed calm and a little sad. He wasn't sure why, but he decided not to dwell on it. There was no sense in waiting, he told her—since he feared changing his mind—and they applied for their marriage license and had their blood tests.

Caught in a whirlwind of numbness, he went by his church alone that afternoon to schedule a wedding date with his pastor. Brother Alan Caldwell, the middle-aged pastor whom Wes believed to be one of the wisest men he'd ever known, also proved to be a little too perceptive.

"This is a joke, right?" he asked when Wes had given him the news. "You're pulling my leg."

"No joke, Alan. It's for real."

The pastor leaned forward on his desk as a slow frown killed his smile. "I didn't even know you were dating anyone."

Wes shifted in his seat. "We haven't been seeing each other for long."

"Well, what's her name? Where did you meet her?"

Wes hesitated. "Her name is Laney Fields."

Alan's face seemed to pale suddenly. "Amy's real mother? The woman who took you to court for custody?"

"The same," Wes said. "Our relationship has . . . changed."

Alan studied his face, and Wes felt as if every lie in his heart sat exposed and ready for dissection. "Wes, you're not doing this out of some noble sacrifice for Amy, are you?"

"Of course not. You saw her in court . . . well, she's beautiful. There's a slight age difference . . . I'm eight years older . . . but she's had a tough life, and she's a lot older inside. And she loves Amy more than anyone else ever could . . ."

"She's definitely beautiful, no question. But she was merciless..."

"It wasn't her," he defended. "It was her attorney. He was the barracuda."

"Still . . ." Alan got up and paced back and forth a moment, a troubled look distorting his face. "That's only been a couple weeks. Wes, you can't expect me to believe that—"

"I do expect you to believe it," Wes cut in impatiently. "Alan, I've been in this church for years, and I feel closer to you than almost anyone in my life. Ever since Patrice died, you've been asking me if you can do anything for me. Well, here I am with something you can do. Perform my marriage ceremony. You do it all the time for people you hardly know. I'm asking you now to do it for me."

Alan propped his foot on his chair and leaned into his knee, his brow wrinkled as he gazed down at his old friend. "But, Wes, are you sure about this? You grieved so hard over Patrice. Sometimes that grief can make us so lonely that we get . . . well . . . desperate to fit someone into the empty slot. And it's only natural that Laney might seem like the right candidate, since she's a factor in yours and Amy's life anyway."

"That's not what I'm doing. It's the right thing to do, Alan. I've given it a lot of thought."

Alan stroked his chin but didn't release Wes from his thoughtful scrutiny. "Have you given it any prayer, Wes?"

Wes couldn't hold his gaze now, so he looked down at the clammy hands he held clasped in his lap. "Yes," he lied.

As if Alan recognized the falsehood, he came around his desk and sat down next to Wes.

"Level with me, Wes, or I can't perform this ceremony. Is she pregnant?"

Wes laughed then, taking Alan by surprise. The absurdity of the question was more than he could stand. "No," he said when he was able. "She's not pregnant."

Alan didn't see the humor and kept his concerned eyes on him until his laughter played out. "You know, usually when someone comes to tell me they're getting married, they come together. I wish you had brought her. I'd like to meet her. She's never even been to church with you."

This was tougher for Wes to evade, so he shifted again and struggled for something that would satisfy Alan. "She'll start coming with me as soon as we're married. And she's not here today because she has so much to do. We want to do it this Thursday. That's when the waiting period will be up."

"But there are so many people who would love to celebrate with you. Don't you want to take more time, plan something bigger, something where you can invite your friends?"

Wes was beginning to get irritated. "No, Alan. We want to do it now."

"And how does Amy feel about it?"

"We're telling her tonight. But it's going to be terrific for her. I can promise you that." His eyes settled on his pastor and with sincerity, he said, "I want you to marry us, Alan, but I'm going through with this whether you do or not."

"Just tell me why you're in such a hurry."

"Because I'm ready to get on with my life. And I'm ready to restore some normalcy to my family. Amy needs that."

"Maybe she does, Wes, but that's not a good enough reason to marry someone. Do you love her?"

Wes met his eyes and felt the hypocrisy and deceit in his heart rising to smother him. "When you meet her, you won't have any questions about this. You'll see immediately why I want to marry her."

"You didn't answer my question," Alan said. "Do you love her?"

Wes couldn't escape those eyes any longer, and for the first time, he wished that Alan wasn't so wise. "I love her as much as I can love anyone after Patrice."

He fully expected for Alan to back out and say that wasn't good enough, but instead, the man sighed heavily. "All right. I'll have to accept that, if you can. But I do have one more question. Is she a believer?"

This one was tougher for Wes, and he shifted again and found something on Alan's desk to fix his eyes on. "She said she would try to accept our faith."

He glanced back at Alan and saw the hope draining out of his face. "She's not, then."

111

"I know what you're thinking," Wes said. "You're thinking that we're unequally yoked. That I'm going against God. But I'm not. I really think God is the one who set this up."

"God doesn't work this way, Wes," Alan said. "If it really was God, he'd give you time to get to know her. Time to fall in love. Time to make sure that you aren't unequally yoked."

"So what are you saying?" Wes asked. "That you won't perform this ceremony? Even though I've told you that I'm going ahead with or without you?"

For a moment, he thought Alan was going to tell him that was exactly the decision he'd made, that it was obvious that God wasn't in this, that if Wes went through with this, he was on his own.

Instead, Alan rubbed his face with his hand and with grieving eyes, looked at his friend. "If I can't talk you into waiting . . ." He took a deep breath. Getting up, he went back to his chair behind his desk, plopped into it, and looked down at his Bible lying open on his desk. "It's not always easy being a shepherd, you know."

Wes didn't answer. He knew where this was going.

"In seminary, they teach you all the right things to do, and all the things not to do. But somehow that gray area always gets left out." He brought his eyes back to Wes's. "If you were the pastor and I was sitting in this chair, telling you that I was marrying an unbeliever whom I didn't even really love, what would you do?"

Wes leaned forward then and set his elbows on his knees. Dropping his head down, he shook his head. "I don't know, Alan. I guess that's why I'm not the pastor. All I know is that this is the best thing for Amy. And that's the only thing that matters to me right now. But if you can't do it, we can always go to the justice of the peace." He got to his feet and slowly started for the door.

But Alan followed him and stopped him before he could reach it. "I'm going to have to trust that you and God have come to terms on this, Wes. And if you're getting married, I don't want it to be by some stranger who doesn't even bring God into it. I'll do the ceremony."

Wes looked up at him, his eyes misty. "Thank you."

"Now sit down, and let's have a look at the calendar."

Slowly, Wes sat back down, and Alan reached for his calendar. "Now, I assume you want to do this in the sanctuary?"

Wes stiffened. "No, not in the church."

Again, those eyes searched him. "Why not?"

"Because. She wants to do it in her backyard." The thought made his heart sink even as he spoke, for he believed in church weddings, but he wouldn't mock God by standing in his house and making a false pledge of everlasting love.

"All right," Alan said, marking that on the calendar. "We can do it wherever you like."

Wes got up to leave, but Alan stopped him before he reached the door. "I'm gonna be praying for you, buddy."

Wes couldn't turn back to look at him. Gazing down at the doorknob in his hand, he said, "Thanks, Alan. I appreciate it."

That night, as nervous as kids about to break a heartbreaking secret to their parents, Wes and Laney told Amy.

"But why?" the child asked as she clutched her teddy bear to her chest—a security toy Wes said she had given up years ago but had found need for again just after her mother's death. "You don't even like each other."

"Yes, we do," Wes argued. "What makes you think we don't?"

Amy gave a dry laugh that made her seem much older than her years. "Because you yell at each other when you think I can't hear. And you give each other mean looks."

Wes glanced at Laney, then down at the floor. "Your mother and I used to fight sometimes, didn't we?" he asked quietly.

Amy shrugged.

"And when we were mad we gave each other mean looks, didn't we? But we still loved each other."

"But you and Laney never kiss."

Their eyes met, then flitted apart.

"Yes, we do," Wes said after a moment. "Just not in front of you."

"Why?"

"Because that's private."

"You and Mommy kissed in front of me."

Wes leaned his elbows on his knees and dropped his head. He had already reached a dead end with Amy, and Laney could see that he lacked the strength to manufacture more lies.

Laney set her hand on his tense shoulder, a gesture meant to comfort all of them. "We will," she lied, "when we're more comfortable with each other. It's just that we thought you wouldn't like it if you saw."

Amy lifted her chin and leveled her eyes on Laney, her directness infinitely less intimidating than the silence she had given her before. "Why do you want to marry my daddy?" she asked perceptively.

Laney thought for a moment. Could she tell her that she wanted to be with her? That it was the only way they could all have what they needed? No, that would put too much pressure on Amy. And it seemed important for her to think this would be a real marriage. Could she admit the warm attraction she felt for Wes, despite his obvious resentment of her? Laney forced a shaky smile and found the only answer Amy would buy. "Because he's handsome and kind and someone I like to be around."

Wes's eyes came up, measured Laney's for honesty, and found it.

Amy seemed satisfied with that. She turned back to her father. "And why do you want to marry Laney?"

Wes kept his eyes on Laney's for a long moment, and he seemed to search himself for the same honesty. "Because she smells good," he said. Laney's heart caught in her throat, and her face grew warm.

Amy wrinkled her nose. "Daddy, that's no reason."

He laughed nervously and considered the question again. When he brought his eyes back to his daughter, they held a gentle yearning, a subtle sadness. "Because I get lonely sometimes, baby."

"And because she's pretty?" Amy prodded, determined to find some logical root to their decision, some root that she could understand.

Wes smiled. "That doesn't hurt any."

Laney found herself matching his smile, despite the fulminating nature of the moment. Their eyes collided, drew apart.

"She's not prettier than my mommy." The words came out on a note of belligerence, and Laney's heart tightened. Wes glanced at Laney, then back at his daughter, obviously at a loss for the right thing to say. "Your mommy was the most beautiful woman in the world, Amy," he said softly.

The child's eyes welled with tears, and she got up and went to the window, staring out into the night. "Sometimes I can't remember what she looks like anymore. I have to go find a picture." She wiped at her tears and turned back to her father. Her words came out quickly, high-pitched and fragile. "Is that why, Daddy? Do you want to marry Laney because you can't remember Mommy?"

Wes got up and grabbed his daughter. Picking her up, he hugged her fiercely. Both of their eyes were closed, but tears still rolled down both their cheeks. Laney watched, frozen and excluded. "Honey, I'll never forget your mommy. Never ever. She was my best girl."

"Then why?" Amy cried harder.

"Because . . ." he whispered. "Because the hardest thing for your mommy was that she knew that when she died, you wouldn't have a mommy, and I wouldn't have a wife. She wanted us to have somebody, sweetheart. She never meant for us to be alone. If she could have stayed with us, she would have, but God needed her home in heaven with him. So he sent us Laney . . ."

Amy buried her face in her daddy's neck and wept. Wes clung to her, allowing her the time to cry out her heart. When a few moments had passed, he whispered, "We want you to be in our wedding, sweetheart. We'll buy you a beautiful dress, and you'll look like a princess. It's going to be good, honey. You'll see. You have to trust us. OK? Can you trust us?"

She nodded slowly, wiping her eyes as he put her down and kissed her cheek. "Can I go to bed now?" she asked.

"Sure. I'll come tuck you in."

"That's OK," she whispered. "Good night."

Laney got to her feet, feeling a little unsteady, as the little girl walked hurriedly toward her bedroom. "Wes, can I go talk to her just for a minute?"

He thought about it, then nodded reluctantly. "Be careful."

She hurried after Amy. The little girl hadn't bothered to disrobe. Already, she had curled up on her bed and lay in a fetal position clutching her teddy.

"Amy?" she asked softly, going to sit beside her on the bed. The little girl didn't answer.

"Amy, I just wanted to tell you that . . . I know how much you loved your mommy. And you know, your mommy is still with you. Her love didn't die with her. It's still here. All around you. And I don't want to take her place or make you forget her. I just want to love you, too."

Amy didn't answer.

"Amy, when you were a baby, I wanted to keep you then. But I was just a teenager, and I didn't have a husband, and my father took you away . . ." Her voice broke, and she tried to go on. "I don't want you to think that I gave you away because I didn't love you. God gave you to the best parents in the world. Your mommy and daddy were so happy to get you. And when your mommy died, I know that her biggest fear was that she would be leaving you without a mother."

Tears rolled out of Amy's eyes, and she closed her eyes to hold them back.

"Amy, I'm not religious like your daddy. I don't really know a lot about God. But I do know that I've prayed over the years that somehow you would be happy and taken care of and that you'd have two parents who loved you. And I've prayed that somehow my pain would go away. Since I've found you, I've believed that God might be answering those prayers. Maybe it really is what your mom would have wanted. Maybe God has worked it all out."

Amy's eyes remained squeezed shut as tears oozed out and rolled across her face.

"Amy, all I know is that I love you more than anything in this world. And in the short time that I've known your daddy, I've come to love him, too. He's a good, kind, sweet man, and I couldn't have picked a better father for you. I want to take care of you both, Amy. I want to keep you both from being lonely, and I want to help you when I can. I want to make your life better, because you've already made my life better. Do you think . . . that maybe you could give me the chance to do that?"

Amy opened her eyes and looked up at Laney. It was hard for her, Laney thought, but she *was* trying. "Do you really think it's OK with Mommy?"

"I think Mommy would have had the idea herself," she whispered. "She knew that no one could love you as much as she could except for your other mother."

The fact that she didn't call herself Amy's "real" mother seemed to help, and Amy thought that over for a moment, sniffing and wiping her eyes. Finally, she whispered, "Do I get to carry flowers at the wedding?"

Laney smiled through her tears. "Yes. Of course."

"I want to carry daisies," Amy whispered. "They were Mommy's favorites."

"We'll get you the prettiest bouquet of daisies anybody ever saw," Laney whispered.

From the hall, Wes listened to what he could hear of the conversation. She was reaching Amy. He leaned back against the wall and thought of what she'd just told Amy about loving him. Some emotion he hadn't expected welled in his throat, and he swallowed it back.

In a moment, Laney came out of Amy's room. She saw Wes standing there and looked up at him. She was crying. "You heard?"

"Yeah," he whispered.

"She's gonna be all right with this," Laney said softly. "She wants to carry daisies."

He smiled painfully as tears sprang to his eyes. He started to speak, but his mouth quivered, and he gave up. Nodding at her to follow, he led Laney out onto his back patio where they could talk without being overheard.

The stars were just beginning to make their debut, and a warm breeze skittered across the yard, bringing with it the scent of freshly mowed lawns and summer flowers.

Except for a child-sized lawn chair, the only other piece of furniture there was a padded swing that seated two. Wes sat down and waited for Laney. She hesitated.

"Come on," he said quietly. "We're going to have to get used to being close to each other."

Close to each other. Did he know, she wondered, that being close to him made her a nervous wreck?

Laney sat down. Their thighs and shoulders brushed, and her heart pounded like an adolescent's. Years had passed since a man had had such an effect on her, and she had believed those nervous feelings were a thing of the past. The swing rocked back and forth with a rhythmic squeak, and Wes leaned his head back.

"The things you said to her . . . they reached her. I think they made her feel better."

She remembered what she'd said about loving Wes and felt awkward. She hadn't known he was listening. Now it hung there between them, like a secret unveiled, an embarrassment they couldn't mention.

"You were right, Laney," he said finally. "This will give her the best of both worlds."

"I know it can," she said.

"She wasn't for it, exactly, but she wasn't against it," he went on.

"I won't push things," she said. "I want to make friends with her first, before I try to be her mother."

"You'll be fine," he whispered.

The masculine scent of his cologne drifted to her senses, and she closed her eyes and savored it. It would be all right, she thought. Marriage to Wes would even be good.

"You realize I want us to live here," he said, breaking into her thoughts. "I know your house is bigger and you just moved back, but this is Amy's home. It's mine too. I'm not ready to turn my back on it yet."

Laney knew what he really meant was that he wasn't ready to turn his back on Patrice. "I understand," she whispered.

"Do you?"

She met his gaze in the darkness. "Yes. And I'll try to make it easy on you."

His eyes canvassed her face gently, and the swing continued to squeak. His green eyes glistened, not with regret this time, not with grief, not with anger or sadness. This time she felt them glisten for her. "And who's going to make it easy on you?" he asked after a while.

Laney caught her breath at his unexpected question. "I never expected it to be easy."

He assessed her for a moment longer, his eyes probing, searching, and then he moved his gaze out over the small lawn. So much was between them, he thought. He felt drawn to her, but that pull made him hold back. They were getting married, yet she knew very little about him. It didn't take a genius to see that she walked on eggshells around him. He had asked her questions bordering on cruelty. She had asked him nothing.

He shifted a little to face her and lifted a strand of her hair, brushing his thumb pensively across the ends. The swing stopped. The wind stilled.

"We found out Patrice had cancer about two years ago," he said in a gravelly voice that told her the words didn't come easily. "When they tried to do surgery they realized it had spread too far. We tried chemotherapy, radiation . . . None of it really helped. It was hard on Amy."

What about him? she ached to ask. Was it hard on him? Was it still hard? Laney kept her eyes on him, and he stared down at the hair sliding over his finger. "How long were you married?" she asked.

"Twelve years," he said.

"Twelve years," she repeated in awe. "To love someone for that long . . ." Her voice faded wistfully, dying on a note of bewilderment.

"It isn't so long," he said quietly. "It wasn't long enough."

"No," she whispered. "I don't suppose it was."

His hand continued stroking her hair, growing more familiar with the softness. "Have you ever loved anyone like that? A man, I mean?"

"That only happens to the lucky ones," she whispered.

"And you aren't lucky?"

She gave a tiny shrug and looked at Amy's bike leaning against the fence.

"Why?" he asked. "Why haven't you married?"

"I couldn't," she said.

"Couldn't?" He wasn't going to let it go at that. There must have been chances. "Were you afraid?"

She kept her gaze distant, fighting the ghosts that didn't have to be a part of her life anymore. "You don't understand."

"No," he agreed. "But if you felt you couldn't marry anyone until me, I'd like to understand. I want to know what makes a woman want to give up any chance she has for that kind of love by tying herself to a man she hardly knows."

Laney took a deep breath and narrowed her eyes against the pain. Her voice was hardly louder than that breath. "Ever since I had Amy it was like I'd put my life on hold. Like a big piece of it was missing, and I couldn't move ahead until I'd found that piece." She looked at him, searching for understanding. "You can't know what it's like. Every time I saw one of those missing children on television or heard of a case of child abuse or saw a mother neglecting a child in a store, I wondered if she was mine. I bought her things, then gave them away. I wrote her letters, then burned them. It almost drove me crazy."

Wes's hand closed over hers. "How did you find her?"

"There was a searcher—a private investigator who specialized, illegally, in this type of thing. I paid him a lot of money, and he got me the records. Once I had your names, the rest was easy."

He took her hand and laid it palm up in his, straightened out her fingers, and stroked the inside of her fingers with his fingertip. She watched, wondering why she wasn't terrified of the contact that was so foreign to her. "What would you have done if Patrice had still been alive? Would you have stopped at just seeing Amy?"

"Yes," Laney admitted adamantly. "At least until she was grown up. But I wanted to be in the same town to be able to watch her from a distance. No one would ever have known."

He closed his eyes and leaned his head back, but, thankfully, kept his hand over hers. "It all seemed so easy when we adopted her. Everybody was a winner, we thought."

"You *should* have thought that," she said. "I wouldn't have wanted Amy raised by people who felt guilty for loving her."

Turning her hand over, she laced her fingers with his. He opened his eyes. "Wes," she whispered intently. "Thank you for working with me on this."

"I'm not working with you, Laney," he said. "I'm marrying you."

The words settled like a soothing caress over her senses, and when he took her chin with his finger and beckoned her closer, she went.

Their lips met tentatively, then withdrew. When the terror in both of them passed, they tested again. He was warm, warmer than she'd ever imagined a man could be. Her hand slowly rose between them to touch his chest. She felt his heart sprinting as the kiss bonded their lonely souls, offering them something more than a child to share.

But that bond through its very warmth was frightening to Laney. She'd never felt that warm. That protected. And it couldn't last. Even his anger had been easier for her to accept. She pulled away and caught her breath. Standing up, she looked nervously down at him. "I have to go now," she said.

"I'm sorry," he said quickly, rising too. "I didn't—"

"Don't," she said, stopping him. "It's OK. I'm just—"

"It's getting late," he cut in.

"A little tired," she finished.

"There's so much to do."

"Yeah."

They stared at each other for a tense moment, then Laney started back into the house. Wes followed her to the door. "Are you OK?"

"Fine," she said too exuberantly. "Yes, fine." She started out the door.

"See you Thursday, then? Or before?"

"Thursday," she said hurriedly. "I'll see you Thursday."

And then, before her heart flew right out of her chest, she got in her car and drove away as fast as the speed limit would allow.

Wes stood in the doorway watching her car lights disappear in the distance. A faint smile softened his features for a moment, the first in a very long time, and he thought that marriage might not be so bad after all. He had kissed her against his judgment, against his own warnings, against every spark of wisdom within him, and he'd been as nervous as a sixteen-year-old kid. It had been a long time since his heart had had such a workout. The last time was . . .

His smile faded as memories of Patrice washed over him like a reprimand. It was too soon for him, he told himself. He had no right. Slowly he closed the door and went to his bedroom.

That night he slept with Patrice's picture clutched against his chest.

CHAPTER ELEVEN

It wasn't the wedding that Laney had dreamed of as a child, but it was a wedding, and as surely as if she were in a cathedral with two thousand guests instead of two witnesses and a little girl who wasn't sure how to react, she was pledging the rest of her life to Wes Grayson and his daughter.

Alan Caldwell did his best to make the no-frills ceremony seem more significant, but the lawn mower next door and the radio playing by her other neighbor's pool robbed it of some of its charm. Laney had chosen to wear white, simply because she had never considered a wedding in any other color, but she had neglected things like flowers and candles when she had prepared for this, except for the spray of baby's breath tucked in one side of her hair and the bouquet of daisies Amy carried in her mother's honor.

Laney had dreaded seeing Wes's sister and facing up to her so-you've-trapped-him scrutiny, but the woman had surprised her. With a flip of her flirty blond curls, she had said, "So here's where Amy got those eyes to die for." And then she had taken Laney's picture with the enthusiasm of a proud sister-in-law. Laney had loved her immediately.

Clint Jessup, Wes's best friend since college, had been another story. When they were introduced, he had barely managed a smile. Laney was left with the distinct impression that the man had done his best to talk his friend out of this nonsense but had grudgingly agreed to be a part of it when he failed. Wes had explained that Clint was soon going to marry Sherry's best friend, the love of his life. The idea of feeling less than total commitment to the institution of marriage had, no doubt, given him reason for concern.

And then there was Amy. Laney had bought her the little white lace dress she wore and had it delivered to Wes's house. She hadn't

123

been sure if Amy would like it or if it would fit, but the fact that Amy had worn it meant everything to Laney. In her hair was a lace bow, lovingly tied, but slightly crooked, and she carried the daisies like a fragile treasure. She was still withdrawn, still quiet, still unsmiling. But she was no longer openly hostile.

Wes was a warm, quiet presence at Laney's side. Their kiss the other night had done a number of things. It had made her heart flutter in anticipation of the marriage itself instead of just motherhood. Laney realized she would have a husband to contend with, and she didn't know if she could deal with that. Why had he kissed her? she had wondered over and over. He barely tolerated her.

Her hand trembled when he slipped the gold band on her finger. His trembled when she slipped his on. Their eyes held a million fears as they faced each other to exchange vows. And when Alan said, "You may kiss the bride," Laney felt her heart fall to her feet.

Wes lowered his head and touched her lips with his, so softly that she felt a surge of disappointment at first. But he didn't withdraw when she expected. Instead he stepped closer and slid his arms around her and breathed in a sigh that stole her breath. And then he gave that breath back to her. His lips moved softly against hers, gently welcoming her to his world despite the conditions. She felt herself running head-first toward the biggest heartbreak of her life, yet she responded to the kiss with a fervor that equaled his. They looked into each other's eyes with a note of surprise when they broke the kiss, then let each other go too quickly.

They had scarcely separated when Sherry threw her arms around Laney, welcoming her to the family, and thrust a wrapped package into her arms. "It's a wedding gift," she said quickly. "I made it for you. I admit it was kind of rushed, so if it falls apart or anything, I'm sorry. Don't open it till you get home." Sherry winked at her brother. "It's for you, too, Wes."

Wes dropped a kiss on his sister's cheek. "Thanks." He turned back to Laney, his smile hesitant. "Is it moving?"

She shook the box. "No."

"Good," he said. "Then it isn't some exotic animal she got from a mail-order catalog. Sherry's taste in gifts has always been questionable. But it's the thought that counts."

Sherry grinned conspiratorially at Clint, who rolled his eyes. "Yeah, and a little thought can lead you a long way," she said.

Clint finally broke into a laugh and told her to quit while she was ahead, and Laney couldn't wait to see what was in the box. It was a day for special gifts. A daughter, a husband, a home. What more could anyone ask for?

L aney thought of a hundred things she'd like to ask for that evening when they had put Amy to bed. Tranquilizers, a cot in the living room, a hole to hide her head in.

What had been a busy day of moving in had now come to a complete halt, and she found herself in the most awkward situation of her life. What did he expect of her? What did she expect of him? Where would she sleep in this two-bedroom house? Where would he *expect* her to sleep?

She looked around the small living room at the family portrait on the wall, at the knickknacks she was sure Patrice had bought, at the color scheme that belonged to another woman. They mocked her now, chiding her for inserting herself into a family where she didn't belong. She wanted to cry, but she was too afraid. She wanted to run, but she was too determined. She wanted to be sick, but she was too embarrassed.

She looked up and saw Wes standing in the doorway, looking at her with his own apparent reservations. If only he looked like an ogre, she thought, hugging her knees to her chest, maybe she could make this cut and dried. If only he didn't have those soft green eyes that made her heart melt, she might not be so afraid. If only she weren't so tragically attracted to him . . .

"I was think—"

"You never ope—"

The words came out simultaneously, and they both stopped. Laney felt her cheeks coloring. She swallowed. "You go ahead," she said. "What were you going to say?"

He walked into the room and sat down next to her. "You never opened Sherry's gift."

She looked at the wrapped package on the coffee table. "Well, I could do it now."

He handed it to her. "Brace yourself. My sister's a real character."

"I like her," Laney said. Her hands trembled as she peeled up the tape, careful not to tear the paper. "I wonder what it is. She said she made it herself."

Wes helped her with one side of the paper then propped his elbow on the back of the sofa and rested his head against his hand, watching her.

She opened the box, pulled back the tissue covering, and found the contents. Her face stung with crimson heat.

"What is it?" Wes asked when she set the top back on too quickly.

"Nothing, it's just . . ."

"Just what?" He smiled and reached for the box. She had no choice but to surrender it to him. "What did my crazy sister do this time?"

He pulled off the top and reached for the black pile of lace. Taking one strap, he held it up. "A negligee," he said, his own face reddening. "That Sherry."

Slowly he folded it back up, set it in the box, and closed it. "Well," he said after what seemed an eternity. "She meant well. She's an aspiring fashion designer, you know. Goes to school part-time. She's always experimenting . . ." His voice trailed off as he realized he was babbling.

Laney swallowed the tears gathering in her throat. "I . . ." She cleared her throat and tried again. "I was thinking. This couch is pretty comfortable. I could sleep here. I mean, I know you've given up a lot already, marrying me and all, and I don't want you to have to give up your bed too. And I don't want you to think that I think that this is a real marriage, because we both know it's for Amy's sake. We don't have to pretend we're attracted to each other or that we have to go through with anything that isn't right for us. I mean, since we hardly know each other . . ."

Wes sat listening, his face expressionless as her words tumbled out. Had he expected it to be any different? Had he really hoped that they would consummate this charade of a marriage tonight?

When her arguments ran down, he looked into her liquid, frightened eyes and hated himself for anything he'd ever done to make her fear him so. "Laney, we got married for Amy. And we want very much for her to think of it as a real marriage. This house has two bedrooms. Mine and Amy's. If either one of us sleeps anywhere but in that bedroom, she'll know. She wakes up early, and sometimes she gets up in the night. If it's going to look like a real marriage, we have to sleep in the same room."

Laney hugged her knees tighter, and her lips trembled. "You're right," she whispered. "I know you're right."

She was shaking all over, he thought miserably. She was scared to death.

She stood up, finally, and looked down at him. "I . . . guess I'll go get ready for bed, then."

Did she think he was going to force her to make love? Did she think he was that insensitive? He stood up to face her. "Laney."

She dropped her face and tried to blink back the incipient tears. "What?"

He took her hand and drew her closer to him. "Laney, you don't have to be afraid of me. I'm not going to take anything from you."

His voice was comforting, gentle, and she made herself look up at him. A tear seeped through her lashes, and his hand moved up to her face. With his thumb he brushed the tear away.

His lips came down to her cheek, kissed the wet spot, melting all her fears and apprehensions, and then withdrew. "I won't touch you again tonight," he whispered.

And when she didn't answer, he dropped her hand and left the room.

Laney's spirits hovered between disappointment and relief when she heard him go into the bathroom and turn on the shower. She went into the bedroom and got ready for bed. The light from the room's one small lamp slid across the long black gown Laney had brought for the occasion. It was not anything that could be considered alluring. It was simply attractive, pleasant to look at—nothing like the negligee Sherry had made her—and she'd justified it by telling herself that she couldn't let her new husband see her in the football jersey she usually slept in.

She slipped under the covers and turned on her side so she would appear to be asleep when Wes came in. But Patrice's picture on the bedside table seemed too threatening. The blond-haired, blue-eyed woman smiling peacefully out from the frame added weight to Laney's heart. The picture was a cold reminder that this would be a marriage in name only. Wes was still in love with his first wife. His real wife.

She turned over and scooted to the opposite side of the bed. Wes probably kept that picture there because that was his side. She had no right to come between him and his memories of his wife. Lying on her back, she laid her wrist over her eyes. *Don't cry,* she ordered herself. *Do not cry.*

She sensed Wes before she saw him in the doorway, clad in a maroon robe and a pair of pajama pants.

"I . . . I didn't know which side you slept on," she said quietly.

"Doesn't matter."

She sat up partially, keeping the covers pulled over her gown. "Yes, it does. I can sleep on either side."

"I'm gonna sleep here . . . on this couch."

She swallowed. "Oh."

She watched him get two blankets from the closet and lay them over the cushions.

"Wes, I can sleep there. This is your bed. I never meant to drive you out."

"Don't be silly," he said. "This is real comfortable. We got it when Patrice was sick, and I slept here for months so she could be comfortable in the bed."

Several moments ticked by.

"About the picture," he whispered finally. "I put it away once, and Amy got upset. I had to put it back. It's going to stay there."

Was it defiance in his voice? A reminder that she would not replace Patrice?

"I understand," she whispered without looking at him.

She heard his steady, self-conscious breathing and the sound of his body shifting on the sofa. She tensed when she heard him get up, held her breath as he seemed to come closer, and opened her eyes in alarm when she felt him reaching over her.

"The light," he said.

She looked up at him, about to say that she could do it, but she couldn't speak. He was gazing down at her, an open struggle going on in his eyes, and for a moment she hoped he wouldn't keep his word about not touching her again. Suddenly she needed very much to be touched.

But after turning out the light, Wes withdrew to the couch, and she closed her eyes again. Laney tried not to think how appealing he looked with his hair damp from the shower. But there was no way to block out that fresh scent of soap that wafted over the air . . .

Wes lay on his back, staring up at the ceiling, willing his senses to ignore the apricot scent that teased him whenever she was near.

Viciously, he turned over on his side and wadded his pillow under his head, wishing he'd never come up with the noble idea of sleeping on this couch.

He ground his teeth and buried his face in the pillow. It was going to be a long night.

CHAPTER TWELVE

For the first time in many months, the smell of coffee woke Wes. Slowly he opened his eyes and stretched as much as he could on the narrow couch. He glanced across at the bed and saw that Laney had gotten up and made it up behind her. She had probably hurried out, he thought, to avoid the intimacy of morning.

Sliding his feet to the floor, Wes sat on the edge of the couch, a little disappointed. He could hear her puttering in the kitchen, and he wondered if she'd slept at all. Had she been too nervous, too tense, too self-conscious to lie there until he woke?

He got up and folded his blankets, hiding the evidence of where he'd slept from Amy. When he stepped into the bathroom, he breathed in the sweet scent of apricots drifting on the steam from Laney's shower. The feminine fragrance reminded him how much he had missed having a woman in his house.

Going back into the bedroom, he pulled open a drawer and grabbed a shirt. It was then that his eyes fell on the check lying on the dresser next to his wallet.

He picked it up, every muscle in his body going rigid. Laney had written him a check for a phenomenal amount of money—enough to pay off Patrice's hospital debts and bail out his home and business. It should have felt like an answered prayer, but instead, it reminded him that their marriage was a business arrangement. Cursing himself for having no choice but to use it, he crammed it into his billfold.

It was his fault her gesture had been so coldly impersonal, he told himself as he got dressed. After all, he was the one who had balked when she'd suggested a joint checking account. He couldn't stand the idea of living off her inheritance when he had nothing of his own to put into the pot. As soon as his business was on its feet, he would pay her back, and he'd never live on her father's money again.

Quickly he dressed, then sat down on the edge of the bed, not ready to face her with the mixed feelings whirling through his heart. Should he thank her or pretend the check hadn't been written?

He looked down at the bed beneath him and ran his hand along the bedspread. She had lain here so still last night, almost as if she held her breath, waiting for him to fall asleep. Some part of him had longed to touch her . . . to reassure her . . . but he hadn't dared. It had been one of the loneliest nights of his life. And this was probably the loneliest morning.

He rubbed his hands roughly over his face then dropped them as his eyes fell on Patrice's picture. He wondered how Laney had felt waking to it this morning. Did it make her feel out of place, in the way? He picked it up and once again tried to put it in the table drawer. But something about that act seemed like a betrayal. He couldn't do it.

He set the picture back, exactly where it had been before, and tried to remember Patrice as she had been at her best, laughing with him and exchanging wisecracks. The house had always been so full of laughter. But the memory was fading, just as Amy had said. Now, as he looked at Patrice's picture, it was Laney's scent he smelled. As he remembered how Patrice had cared for him, it was Laney's work in the kitchen he heard. As he thought of how he'd loved Patrice, it was Laney he longed to touch.

It was wrong, he told himself. All wrong.

He heard the sound of a small knock on the door, and he said, "Come in."

The door opened, and Amy peered in. "Hi, Daddy." Her cheeks were sleepy-red, her eyes were just-opened, and she stood in her baby-doll gown with her teddy crushed against her. "Something smells good."

"Laney's cooking breakfast," he said.

She stood there for a moment, looking at him with as much confusion about this change in their family as he felt. "Wanna come?" she asked.

Slapping on his smile, he said, "I sure do. I'm starved."

Taking hands, they both went into the kitchen with quiet apprehension.

Laney had the table set and was putting a platter of French toast at the center of the table. "Good morning," she said, her face lighting up at the sight of her daughter. "You hungry?"

Amy nodded and pulled out a chair.

"Let me just get the syrup, and we'll be all set," Laney said.

"I'll help," Wes said, and followed her.

Laney gave him a puzzled look. She reached for the syrup, then awkwardly handed it to him.

It was sticky, but he didn't notice. He looked down at it and seemed to study it as he tried to find the words. "Uh . . . I saw the check. It was too much."

"You'll need extra until you get on your feet. Really, I want you to have it."

He looked up at her, at the bright, clear, dark eyes that were so stunning at this hour of morning. "Look, I'm going to pay you back. As soon as I get that contract for the amusement park . . . if I get it . . . I'll pay back every penny. With interest."

"I don't need it back. It was a gift. Amy's inheritance. It meant the world to me to be able to do it. I've never had anything I could give before."

He stiffened. "I'm still paying it back."

She wilted and took the syrup from him, then handed him a wet towel for his hands. "Wes, how can I make you understand? I've never been able to do anything for her. Or for you, and all these years, you've taken care of my child. Besides, that was the deal. I got what I wanted, and you got what you needed."

"What I *need* is to provide for my family, Laney. It's what I do. I also always try to pay my debts, if it's at all in my power."

"But we're married, Wes. If we get a joint account, it'll all be yours, anyway. What difference will it make?"

He rubbed the back of his neck and shook his head. "I told you, we're not getting a joint account. I'm not ready for that."

He left the kitchen, and she stood there for a moment, trying hard not to cry. She had to go in there and face Amy like the happy little bride. If it killed her, she would do it. Wes hadn't meant to hurt her, she told herself. But he had no idea how much it had meant to her to give what she had to the man who had raised her child. He couldn't possibly understand that the gift had been from her heart— not something she would hold over his head.

Only time could prove that to him, she thought. But she had time. Time to change his mind about the money . . . and time to change his feelings about her.

Nothing changed in their relationship over the days that followed. Amy remained polite but quiet. Laney remained warm but distant. And Wes didn't get much sleep.

Sunday morning, they got up with every intention of going to church together, despite Laney's fears that she wouldn't be well received by the congregation who knew she was the woman who had sued for joint custody of Amy. She knew they'd all be suspicious of the quick wedding.

But she determined to show them just what a nice family they all made. She had bought Amy a new dress for the occasion, and Amy, grouchier than usual, had fidgeted while Laney tried to French braid her hair. When Laney was halfway finished, Amy began to whine. "I don't like it," she said. "It hurts. It's pulled too tight."

"I can loosen it," Laney said. "Here, let me—"

But Amy began to pull it loose herself, destroying the look. "I don't want to wear it like this. I want to wear it down."

Looking a little disgruntled, Laney pulled out the braid and brushed Amy's hair. "That better?" she asked.

"No," Amy pouted. "I want it pulled back. With a bow."

Laney gathered it at her neck to make a ponytail, but Amy jerked away. "Not like that!"

When Amy had begun to cry, Wes intervened. "Come on, short stuff. You're giving the lady a hard time."

"She doesn't know how to fix my hair, Daddy!" Amy whined. "You do it."

Dejected and blinking back her tears, Laney handed him the bow she had bought to go with the dress. "It's OK, Wes," she said. "I need to go get ready anyway."

He nodded and watched her leave, wishing he knew what to say to take that look of absolute rejection off of her face. "You should really go easier on her, kiddo," he told his daughter. "She was just trying to make you look pretty."

"I don't want her to make me look pretty," she grumbled. "I hate that dress she bought me."

"Well, you're going to wear it." He lowered his voice and made Amy look at him. "Honey, Laney's a little nervous this morning. She's not used to going to church. We have to make her understand how much Jesus loves her and wants her there. Now, if we get her all upset and more nervous before we go, she may not ever have the chance to get to know Jesus. So will you try not to be a pain?"

Amy thought that over for a moment, then sighed. "But Daddy, that dress."

"It's beautiful, Amy, and it makes you look like a princess."

"It's stupid. I hate all those ruffles. My friends will make fun of me."

"No, they won't. They'll all beg their moms for dresses just like it."

He finished her hair and turned her around. The bow was a little crooked, as usual, and he tried to adjust it. "Laney could do a much better job at this." He smiled at her, tipping his head. "Do you realize you look just like her?"

Amy didn't quite know how to take that. So she shrugged.

"That's a compliment," he whispered. "Laney's beautiful. And so are you."

A reluctant smile tugged at her lips. "No, I'm not."

"Yes, you are. Modeling scouts will probably interrupt the service to take your picture. Movie directors will run into the sanctuary from the street, after hearing about the seven-year-old beauty who sits inside. And I'll bet Prince Wills will make a special trip from England to come and check you out himself."

Amy giggled. "Oh, Daddy."

"Really," he said. "Now go put the dress on. And step into it, so you don't mess up your hair."

She started back to her bedroom then thoughtfully turned around. "Daddy? Maybe I will let Laney do my hair again."

"Good move, sweetheart. If you're going for the total look, you definitely need Laney."

Wes hadn't known what to expect when they walked into the church as a family, but he hadn't exactly expected the cold stares aimed at his new wife. Some of his friends, the ones who had not gotten the news off of the grapevine, didn't know about the wedding and looked hurt that he had not told them and startled that the woman he'd married was the barracuda who had taken him to court for his daughter.

He had tried to avoid introducing her to Eugenia Stairs, the church's most active busybody, but she had made a beeline for them the minute she spotted them.

"Tell me it isn't true," the woman spouted off to him. "You're *not* married, are you?"

Wes touched the small of Laney's back and smiled. "Eugenia, this is my wife, Laney. Laney, I'd like you to meet—"

"Wes," the woman cut in, ignoring Laney completely. "I wish you'd called me before you did this. Maybe I could have talked you out of it!"

Wes glanced at Laney. She was taking it all gracefully, though her expression looked as fragile as a porcelain doll's. "Eugenia, why on earth would you want to talk me out of it?"

"Because it's so obvious, Wes."

Wes set his arm around Laney and guided her around Eugenia. "Excuse me, Eugenia, but we're going to find a seat now."

"Well, is she going to join the church?"

Wes turned back. "She isn't deaf, Eugenia. She hears very well. You don't have to talk as if she isn't here. And as for her joining the church—" He glanced at Laney and saw her staring at the floor. Suddenly he felt very protective of her. She was breakable, and he didn't want to see these people hurt her anymore. "The fact is, Eugenia, that she'd have to be crazy to join a congregation that has been so incredibly rude to her. In fact, if it continues, we'll probably all find a new church."

"Oh, Wes! We certainly didn't mean to be rude. If I've offended you, I apologize!"

"Don't tell me," Wes bit out. "My wife is the one you were rude to."

For the first time, Eugenia looked directly at Laney and lifted her chin high. "I'm terribly sorry," she said in a clipped voice. "I didn't mean to be rude to you. Everyone is welcome in our church."

Laney swallowed and tried to smile. "Thank you."

But Wes knew that she didn't believe it. To her, God's house probably seemed to be populated with a bunch of holier-than-thous who knew nothing of the sacrifices Laney had made to be a part of his family.

As they took their place in the pew, Wes sat between Laney and Amy. Reaching over, he took Laney's hand in his. "I'm so sorry about that," he whispered. "About all of them. They're usually very nice people."

"It's OK," Laney said. Tears were in her eyes as she looked at him, and she tried valiantly to keep them back. "They all knew and loved Patrice. And they love you and Amy. They have every right to be suspicious of me. I'm the one who's made your life miserable for the last several months."

He sighed and squeezed her hand tighter. "They'll come around, Laney. I know they will. This isn't a rejection of you."

"I know," she whispered. "I really do know that."

As the sermon began, Wes kept holding her hand, a small reassurance that he, at least, was on her side.

Even though Wes aligned himself with Laney against the friends who had known him for years, it didn't make things easier for Laney and him. It was odd, how hard it was for him to show her any affection at all when Amy wasn't around. It was as though he had to pretend she didn't move him at all when they were alone. It wasn't until Amy was around that he felt he could relax and really enjoy Laney's presence. It should have been the other way around. He was supposed to be acting when they were *with* Amy. He found the paradox confusing.

The following Tuesday, Laney called him at work.

"They called from school," she said in a rush. "Amy's sick. She's got a fever!"

"Just calm down," he said. "Do you know where the school is?"

"Of course I know where the school is!" she blurted. "I've already picked her up. She's burning up. I have to get her to the doctor!"

He leaned over his desk and tried to stay calm. "Have you taken her temperature?"

"Her temperature? Oh, I didn't even think . . . Where do you keep the thermometer?"

"It's in the bathroom medicine cabinet. Laney—"

The phone went dead, and Wes stared at it. Quickly he dialed his home number.

After several rings Laney picked it up. "Hello?" she shouted.

"Laney, why did you hang up?"

"I had to get the thermometer!"

Wes stood up and began shoving things in his desk drawer. "Is it in her mouth?" he asked, keeping his voice steady.

"Yes, it's in her mouth. Was I supposed to do it under her arm?"

Her panic began to register in him, and it was contagious. "No, her mouth is good. There's nothing you can do for at least three minutes, so I want you to calm down."

He heard her taking deep breaths. "OK," she said. "I'm calm."

"It's probably just the flu," he said. "It's been going around her school, but it wouldn't hurt to get her checked. The name of her pediatrician and the number are beside the phone. Do you see it?"

"Yes, I see it." Why did she sound like someone who'd been thrust into the pilot's seat of a descending airplane? "I'll make an appointment as soon as I see what her temperature is."

"I think it's time now," he reminded her.

He waited while she read the thermometer. She gasped. "Oh, no!"

His stomach flip-flopped. "What is it?"

"It's 101."

Wes rolled relieved eyes to the ceiling. "It's OK," he said. From the sound of Laney's voice, he'd expected at least 106. "She's had higher. She'll be fine. Just give her some Tylenol and take her in."

"Tylenol. Of course." She swallowed. "Wes, I'm sorry to bother you with this at work. It's just that I didn't—"

"I'll come home if you think—"

"No," she said quickly. "I can handle it. I'm fine. Thanks. I have to go now."

Wes listened as she cut them off again. Slamming down the phone, he reached for his car keys and started for the door. Laney was not equipped to deal with a sick child, and he wasn't equipped to trust her to. "I'm going home," he told Sherry. "Amy's sick. She has to go to the doctor."

"I heard." Springing to her feet, she followed him to the door. "Wes, let Laney handle it," she said. "Give her a chance."

"I don't take chances with my daughter."

"Wes, I heard you tell her the flu was going around. What good will it do for you to rush home like a crazy person?"

"What harm will it do?" he flung back at her.

"Plenty. It'll tell Laney that you don't trust her, it will tell Amy that you're overly concerned, and it'll make you late getting this bid in that could pay both our electric bills for the next ten years if the amusement park contract doesn't come through. Laney's money may have bailed us out, but it won't keep us in business. This bid will. Need more reasons?"

Wes looked into his sister's bright eyes and wondered where she got all the wisdom she'd been raining on him for the past few months. It seemed like only yesterday that he was climbing a tree to rescue her when she got her hair tangled on a limb. With a defeated sigh, he dropped his keys back into his pocket. "You're right."

"Of course I'm right. Everything will be fine."

Wes went back to his office, jingling his keys nervously in his pocket. Sherry was right. Laney could take care of Amy. He sat down and tried to concentrate on all the areas where she'd proven competent so far. Already she had made his life easier. Her meals filled the house with a homey scent that made him look forward to going home. Her sweet way of caring for Amy had given him a peace he hadn't known since Patrice died. Her shy smiles touched him and made his senses come alive.

He looked back down at the blueprint on his drafting table and picked up his pencil. He had nothing to worry about. But he would call every half hour until she got back just to make sure.

When Laney seemed distracted on the phone after the visit to the doctor and reluctant to talk to him because she wanted to get back to Amy, Wes decided to go home early after all. He found Laney in Amy's room, sitting on the bed next to the sleeping child, washing her forehead with a damp washcloth.

"How is she?" he asked in a whisper.

Laney looked up. Her mascara was smudged beneath her eyes, and her skin looked paler than Amy's. "She's got the flu. The doctor gave her a shot, but he said it would have to run its course."

He sat down gently on the bed next to her. His fresh, masculine scent softened the air that had grown stale in the sick child's room, and the way Laney's senses responded made her angry.

"Does she still have a fever?" he asked quietly.

Laney shook her head with frustration. It was all so useless. Motherhood, marriage . . . she was hopelessly inept. "It's gone up," she said. "I don't know how to get it down."

Wes touched his daughter's forehead with gentle hands. "How high?"

"A hundred and two."

"Well," he said, taking the washcloth from her and setting it on Amy's neck. "It looks to me like you're doing all you can for now. Has she had anything to drink?"

Laney shook her head. "I can't make her drink. All she wants to do is sleep."

"That's OK, too," he assured her. "Why don't you let me take over for a while? Calm down. It's OK."

The tenderness in his voice made her want to scream. It was as if he realized how inept she was and was trying not to point it out. "Wes, would you please stop telling me to calm down?" she whispered. "I *am* calm! I'm just worried!"

"But it's just the flu."

Laney straightened her backbone indignantly. "My daughter is sick. She's miserable, and there's nothing I can do about it! You even rushed home to make sure I had the sense to take care of her. How do you expect me to act?"

"That isn't why I rushed home," he lied. "I just thought you might need help."

"You thought I was falling apart," she told him. "You thought I'd be a basket case!"

"Well, you have to admit you sounded a little panicky."

"I *was* panicky!" She wasn't making any sense, and she knew it. Sighing wearily, she gave him a weak smile. "You're right. I *am* a basket case."

The corners of his lips twitched. "I didn't say that," he reminded her. "You did. I told you you're doing fine."

Laney stood up. "I'm not doing fine. I'm not doing anything." She sniffed and took a deep breath. "Maybe you should take over for a while."

"OK," he whispered. Wasn't that what he'd just said?

"I'll be in the den." Before he could answer, she bolted from the room.

Wes looked down at his sleeping daughter. Her cheeks were flushed with fever, but she was sleeping soundly. The temperature wasn't high enough to be considered dangerous, and there was nothing more he or Laney could do for a while.

He reached over and dropped a kiss on her warm little face. She smelled like Laney, fresh and sweet, though her hair was mussed with sleep. Warmth surged through him, a warmth caused by the apricot scent he had come to associate with Laney and those infantile features that made his daughter a miniature version of her mother. Amy would break his heart someday when she found some punk to marry who would never be good enough for her. He wondered if Laney would break his heart too. Quietly he slipped out of the bedroom and went to the den, expecting to find Laney in a better state than she had been moments earlier.

Instead, he found her hunched in a ball on one end of the sofa, hugging her knees to her chest. Her shoulders shook with the force of her tears.

Quietly Wes went to the couch and sat down next to her. "Laney, what is it?"

She shook her head, unable to answer.

He put his hand on the back of her head, letting his fingers run through her silky hair. Why was it so easy for him to reach out to her when she was broken? "Don't cry," he whispered. "Please."

Something in his tone forced her to look up at him. Her eyes were red and swollen, proof that the tears came from something far deeper than frustration over a sick child.

"Laney, why are you crying?"

She stretched out her palm. "She needs me. She finally needs me, and there's nothing I can do. It's so obvious."

He sighed and tucked her under his arm, pulling her head against his chest. It felt so good to hold her. Why did he have to wait until he had a reason? He closed his eyes and set his chin on her head. She seemed to relax a little in his arms.

"But you've done a lot. You picked her up from school, you took her to the doctor, you put her to bed, and you've been trying to get her fever down. I wouldn't have done things any differently."

"You wouldn't have fallen apart, either," Laney said.

"You're not broken in yet," he told her with a smile. "You're entitled to fall apart now and then. I did it all the time when she was a baby."

Laney wiped her face and brought her dark, liquid eyes back to his. "Really?"

"Of course." He met her eyes and realized how close they were. It felt right, holding her, wiping the tears from her eyes, coaxing the misery out of her. His voice had a lulling quality that was both seduction and security at the same time. "I remember the time her pacifier fell on the floor and my sister put it right back in her mouth. I actually called the doctor in a panic with visions of lethal germs getting into her mouth. He thought I was crazy, I'm sure, but he didn't laugh."

Laney's eyes stole across the room to the family portrait on the wall, to the picture of the baby cradled in her mother's arms. She sniffed. "Amy used a pacifier? I always wondered about that."

"Yes. And she had a favorite blanket that she dragged everywhere. She left it one year in Gulf Shores, Alabama, when we were vacationing. She was about three."

"What kind of blanket was it?"

Wes tilted his head and looked at her, baffled. "Why?"

"I just . . . I've tried to picture her so many times. I lost so much. I know I can't fill it all back in, but it helps to know as much as I can."

His soft eyes swept over her face, and affection danced through them. "It was crocheted. Pink." He watched her absorb the detail, almost as if she were picturing it, as her gaze drifted back to the portrait. "What else do you want to know?"

The tears were beginning to subside, and her eyes brightened with curiosity. "How old was she when she took her first steps? When did she start talking? What were her first words?"

He smiled. "Well, I'd have to look up the first steps. Patrice kept a baby book with all that stuff. But I remember her first word. It was 'uh-oh.' What else?"

"Her first tooth?"

Wes chuckled. "We'll have to look that one up, too. I'm not sure."

Laney sat up, anxious eyes searching his expression. "You have it all written down?"

His eyes held a sweet understanding, and his voice was placating. "Of course. Patrice recorded everything. And we have about ten photo albums. Do you want to see them?"

"Yes," she whispered, feeling as if she'd just been offered her dream with a bow tied around it.

Wes was back in an instant with a stack of albums. He watched as she studied each picture, poignant sadness mingled with tender joy on her face. He answered her questions, told her stories about different snapshots, relayed accidents and events that had colored Amy's young life. Every few minutes Laney would stop to go and check on Amy, and then she was back at his side, laughing with him, misting up now and then, as he helped her learn about her daughter.

And as Laney learned about Amy, Wes learned about her. But the knowledge tugged at his senses, making it harder to keep his distance, making it more and more difficult to remain detached. Laney Fields

Grayson was etching herself on his heart, forging herself into his life, and he found himself feeling good about it. Somewhere along the way they had crossed the threshold between tolerance and affection.

Amy awakened several times that night, and they coaxed her into drinking cold beverages, but around two a.m., she began to cough so violently that she couldn't catch a breath. Laney held her and pounded her back, trying to clear her lungs. "She can't breathe!" she shouted to Wes.

"The shower!" he said over the hacking. "Get her into the bathroom."

"We can't give her a shower now!" Laney cried. Wes grabbed her arm and pulled them behind him.

"The steam," he said, turning on the hot water and closing them into the tiny bathroom. "It'll open her up."

"Oh. The steam." Laney sat on the floor with Amy in her lap and watched the room fill with steam. How had he gotten so smart? she wondered breathlessly. Would there ever be a day when parental decisions came as easily to her? Slowly the croupy coughing subsided, and Amy began to breathe better. So did Laney.

Wes stroked his daughter's hair back from her damp face and smiled as she laid her head limply on Laney's shoulder. "She's going to be fine," he whispered. "Let's get her back to bed."

When they were back in the bedroom, Amy started to cry. "My throat hurts," she rasped.

Before Wes could reach her, Laney had her back in her arms. She took her to the rocking chair and began to sing. The song had a folk flavor, a soft, slow beat that lulled Amy to sleep. He listened, captivated, until the song was over and Amy was breathing easily. "You need to get some sleep," he whispered over Amy. "Why don't you come back to bed?"

Laney looked down at the little girl sleeping so comfortably in her lap. "No, I'll just stay here a while longer."

Disappointment and a feeling very close to jealousy crept through him. He'd felt so close to Laney tonight, sharing the baby pictures with her, warming to her genuine interest when anyone else in the world would rather have been shot than go through a stack of family albums. He wanted more of that warmth for himself. He wanted-ed to lie next to her, slip his arms around her, maybe even see how she'd react if he showed her how much he wanted her. He was afraid, he admitted. It had been a long time since he'd courted a woman. What if she rejected him?

Then sadly, it occurred to him that this parody of a marriage they had entered into was the very thing that would keep him from courting her. They had skipped the steps that might have led to love. They had bypassed God's work in their lives, thinking that he worked too slowly or that he would make the wrong choices in their futures. Laney didn't know God; she had the excuse of ignorance. But Wes knew better. And now he realized that his punishment might be to live trapped in a fake marriage with a burgeoning but inexpressible love. For if he acted on it, when he knew in his heart that the marriage had been neither planned nor blessed by God, wouldn't that be the height of mockery?

But none of it mattered tonight, he told himself, because she wasn't coming to bed. She and Amy needed each other now.

He went to the bedroom and, with great difficulty, finally fell asleep on the couch. He dreamed of sleek black hair, tanned skin, and the subtle scent of apricots. He woke in the middle of the night in a sweat, more tired and frustrated than before he'd gone to bed. The digital clock said four a.m., and still Laney was not in bed.

He got up and went barefoot to Amy's room and felt his heart swelling. Laney was asleep in the rocker, her head resting on Amy's head, and her arms entwined around the sleeping child with a tightness that would have given an orphaned street child a sense of security. He stepped into the room, felt Amy's head, and saw that her fever had broken. Laney, exhausted from the intense vigil, didn't stir when he took Amy from her and laid her in bed.

Then he lifted Laney into his arms. She stirred only enough to see what was happening then laid her head against his shoulder and closed her eyes again. It was as if his holding her was perfectly natural—as natural as her maternal embrace of Amy, as natural as a husband's embrace of his wife.

He laid her carefully in the bed, covered her, then lay on top of the bedspread next to her. She curled up facing him, and fell rapidly into a sound sleep. He reached out and touched her face. Was he falling in love with her? Could it happen so soon? He slid his hand down her shoulder and leaned over to drop a kiss on her forehead, but her rhythmic breathing wasn't interrupted. He slid his arms around her, basking in the strange feelings of contentment coursing through him. When would they cross this threshold between living in a pseudo marriage and thriving in a real one? Would God forgive him for taking matters into his own hands and smile down on this fragile love that was blossoming between them? he asked silently.

Would Patrice?

But there was no answer. Only the gentle sound of Laney's breathing. Only the growing guilt of his lonely heart.

CHAPTER THIRTEEN

Emotions ran high over the following weeks, and every hope Laney had dared to hope was shattered, one by one. She had hoped that her relationship with Amy would be stronger when she'd overcome the flu. Instead, the child emerged from her illness with the same lukewarm tolerance if not outright contempt that she'd had before. She had hoped that the night Wes had shared baby stories with her had somehow bound them, but as he grew more distant and more irritable with each passing day, she realized she had only imagined the tenderness in his eyes. Both Amy and Wes were beginning to see her as an unwelcome addition to their family, she feared, and no matter how hard she tried, she wasn't able to change that.

Wes and Laney spent their evenings speaking to each other in monosyllables, and Wes would rather do almost anything than look her in the eye. He seemed angry at her, as if the night she'd sat up with Amy had somehow changed things. Since he'd gotten the contract for the amusement park, he spent longer days at work and even started working on weekends. At night as she lay in bed and he lay on the couch, he tossed and turned and wadded his pillow, as if the very thought of sleeping in the same room repulsed him.

And neither of them slept. Laney would lie awake, pretending to be asleep, waiting for his breath to settle into its peaceful cadence before she would surrender to sleep. But it never did. So they did battle with each other, both feigning sleep, neither reaching it completely, and both waking with shadows under their eyes and chips on their shoulders. And all the while Patrice's picture sat like a taunting phantom on the table next to the bed.

Laney's spirits were flat and battered one Saturday when she felt herself being sucked into a rare argument with her daughter about the cereal she was having for breakfast. The child was picking a fight, she realized, and she refused to be drawn in. She tried to appease Amy, virtually by giving in to her demands. When Amy "accidentally" dumped her cereal into Laney's lap, Laney didn't allow herself to lose her temper. But Amy kept at it. Her next argument was over the clothes she wanted to wear, an outfit that was being washed at that very moment, but Amy demanded she miraculously dry and dress her in it within the next five minutes. When Laney insisted that she wear something else at the price of a major tantrum, she realized they had to get out of the house.

At the grocery store Amy threw fits over every sugar-sweetened product known to ruin the teeth and temperaments of small children. Laney tried to compromise and bought her some of what she asked for, just to avoid a scene, but even that didn't settle the child down. At the checkout Amy began begging for a candy bar. When she told the child no, an embarrassing scene followed. She wound up carrying Amy out of the store kicking and screaming—terrified she'd get arrested again for kidnapping—and deposited her in the car along with her purse before she set the bags in the trunk. The crying and shouting stopped. Laney breathed a prayer of thanks. And then she went to get in the car.

Amy had locked her out, and the child sat with her arms crossed, staring at the glove compartment, absolutely refusing to let Laney in. Laney tried pleading. Amy ignored her. She tried threatening. Still nothing. And finally, when she was considering breaking a window, a kindly older woman in a post office uniform offered to help. Amy assumed the woman was a police officer, and at her first request she opened the door immediately.

Laney didn't speak to Amy all the way home, but when they were in the house she took her by the hand and led her to her bedroom. There she would sit, she told her, until her father got home. Then she went to the den and cried as Amy shouted her hatred in volumes that reverberated throughout the house. When Amy finally exhausted her verbal abuse and fell asleep on her bedroom floor, Laney seriously considered that her existence in the child's life might, indeed, be a mistake.

Wes came home earlier than usual that day and caught Laney in a hump on the couch.

"What are you doing here?" she snapped.

"I live here," he said.

"But you're early. It's only four."

"But it's Saturday."

"Oh," she said sarcastically, "you noticed that, did you?"

He sat down and frowned. "Yes, I noticed. Why?"

"Why what?"

"Why do I get the feeling I've done something wrong?"

"How can you do anything wrong?" she asked. "You're never here. I wouldn't have a clue whether you've done anything wrong or not!"

"Did you have something you needed me to do today? Is that it?"

"No, Wes. I wouldn't ask a thing of you. I never have."

Dead end, he thought. She was mad at him, and he had no idea why. "Where's Amy?"

Laney stood up. "She's in her room. Being punished." She crossed her arms and jutted her chin defiantly. "Go ahead, Wes. Yell at me. I punished Amy! Do *you* hate me, too?"

"What did she do?"

Laney began to tremble. "What *didn't* she do? She had three bowls of cereal, none of which she liked; she dumped the last one in my lap, cursed me for not being able to miraculously dry her favorite dress in five minutes, made a public spectacle out of us at the grocery store, and locked me out of my own car until a complete stranger came up and told her to let me in!"

Wes nibbled his lower lip. "Oh."

"Oh?" she shouted. "Oh? Is that all you have to say?"

"Well, what do you want me to say, Laney?"

She took a deep breath and forced herself to be strong. She wanted to know if he held her in such contempt, if he, too, rued the day she had walked into their lives. "What do you think, Wes? As dismal failures go, how do you rate me?"

"Laney, I'm not going to tell you you're a failure. You're—"

"I'm *worse* than a failure!" she cried. "My father was right. Go ahead, say it. He was right. I'm completely inadequate as a mother and as a wife. You hate me and Amy hates me and—"

"Wait a minute," he said, catching her flailing arms. "Who said I hate you?"

She jerked away from him and backed across the room, her face glowing with pain and rage. "Nobody has to say it, Wes! All I have to do is look at you. You avoid me. You hardly speak to me. At night you lie on that couch and beat your pillow up." She clutched her head. "I don't know how much more I can expect the two of you to take!"

"So what do you want?" he asked, suddenly angry at the direction her ranting was taking. "Do you want to leave? Is that what you're saying?"

"Is that what you want? Is that what Amy wants?" she shouted, desperate for him to beg her to stay but certain he wouldn't.

"What if it is? Will you run out just like that because things are a little tough? If that's all the backbone you have, then go ahead! Just leave!"

"You'd like that, wouldn't you?" she shouted back. "Maybe that's what all this is about. Maybe you just thought you could run me off by making it as hard as possible. But I don't quit loving my daughter just because she tells me she hates me! I don't quit wanting to know her just because she has a bad day! And I don't back out of my marriage just because my husband avoids me like the plague! I'm not leaving, Wes! I'm staying!"

"Good!" he bellowed.

As if she didn't hear, Laney went on. "And you can scream at me for punishing her if you have to. But when a child misbehaves, she should be punished. I believe that!"

"So do I!" he shouted back.

"Then why are you yelling at me?"

"Because you're yelling at me!"

They stood staring at each other for a long moment, and finally a slow, mischievous smile traveled like sunshine across his face. "Are we finished yelling?" he asked.

She let herself absorb the neat tuck of his shirt, his hands hooked in the belt loops of his pants, his wind-ruffled hair. He looked better than he had a right to, especially when she was standing there with mascara smeared under her eyes.

"Yes, we're finished," she said, trying but failing to return his smile. "But nothing's solved. Amy still hates me, I still punished her, and you'd probably like nothing better than to have never met me."

Wes shook his head from side to side in a what-am-I-going-to-do-with-you gesture.

Stepping toward her, he gazed down at her red eyes. "It was an endurance test, Laney," he said. "Amy was testing you. Don't you see? In her own way she was trying to see how far she could push you and how much of a parent you really are. You passed."

"I did?"

His hand came up, hovered over her cheek without touching, and his smile slowly faded. When his fingers finally made feather-light contact, she saw him swallow. "Yes, you did. And as for me"—his lips began a slow journey down to hers—"well, I'm starting to get used to you."

She looked up into his luminous emerald eyes that seemed to contain both comfort and terror at the same time. Would he hurt her, she wondered, by taking her heart when he couldn't give his in return? Would he make her love him only to realize she'd always have to battle the ghost of his first wife?

"Then why do you beat your pillow every night?" she whispered.

He ran his thumb across her bottom lip and wet his own. "It's a little complicated," he said.

They looked at each other for a fulminating moment, black, wistful eyes trying desperately not to be wistful, jade, desiring eyes trying desperately not to desire. They both failed as their lips came slowly together.

Wes's arms slid around her, drawing her close as they came together like old lovers who'd been kept apart.

"Daddy?"

Amy's voice from her bedroom startled them, but Wes didn't let Laney go. "What, honey?" His voice was a breathless vibration against Laney's lips.

"Can I come out now?"

"No, honey."

"But why?"

"Because I'm kissing Laney," he said, and then his mouth closed over hers again. She melted in his arms, but silence from Amy's bedroom cooled her ardor after a moment. As difficult as it was, Laney broke the kiss. "Wes," she whispered breathlessly against his face. "It's time for her to come out. I want to go talk to her. I made her something."

His eyes held worlds of frustration, but he reluctantly released her. She stood looking at him, almost shyly, before she darted to Amy's bedroom.

Wes listened impatiently as Laney had a talk with Amy that would have put most mothers to shame. And he watched as she pulled out a little book she had made for Amy, a picture book—pictures of her own and some she had pulled from the photo albums—that held the story of Laney's plight and Amy's adoption and the years between then and the present. He saw the pain on her face as she recounted the years, the tenderness as she spoke of Patrice, the warmth as she spoke of him. He saw Amy's interest in, and her grudging respect of, the woman who was determined to be her mother, and he saw her need to be alone with the book.

But it was nothing like his need to be alone with Laney. While Laney was clearing the dishes from the supper table, Wes slipped to the bedroom and called Sherry. "Hey, Sis," he said quietly. "Are you working at the restaurant tonight?"

"No," she said. "I'm off. I'm working on my designs."

"How'd you like an overnight guest?"

"You?" she asked hesitantly.

"No, Amy."

He could imagine Sherry's smile. "What's the matter, Wes? Want to be alone with your wife?"

"I knew you'd like that," he said. "You can pick Amy up at seven."

"I might make it before that," Sherry told him delightedly.

Grinning, Wes hung up the telephone.

Sherry was there in fifteen minutes, rounding up Amy's things like a whirlwind and announcing that she had two tickets to a hot animated flick and that they planned to make it an all-nighter. Laney was so surprised that she didn't know what to say. When she checked to make sure Amy had everything and found that the child had packed the album Laney had made her, along with her favorite doll, she decided time away was just what Amy needed.

But as soon as the door closed, she was stricken with a sudden rush of fear. She and Wes had never been in this house without Amy. That kiss still hung between them like something unfinished.

"Well," she said uneasily. "That was a surprise."

Wes's eyes held a serious glint. "Not to me, it wasn't." He stepped toward her with the slow, patient purpose of a man with a mission.

"No?" Her voice cracked. "Why not?"

"Because I'm the one who suggested the whole thing. I called Sherry while you were cleaning up."

Tension shimmied along her nerves at his touch, and he slid his calloused hands up her arms to her shoulders and stopped at her neck. She shivered. "Why?"

"Because," he said in a deep voice. "I thought it would be nice if we spent some time alone together."

CHAPTER FOURTEEN

Y ou . . . you don't have to do this," Laney whispered, clinging desperately to the shields that protected her.

"Yes, I do. Believe me, I do."

"But . . . Wes . . . if you think you owe me something, you don't. Our arrangement is fine with me." Her gaze gravitated to the family portrait that had haunted her, to the blond woman who had won Wes's heart first, then left it aching because she had no choice. "Besides . . . your memories. They're everywhere. They're part of you. I don't want you to try to feel something for me that you just can't feel."

His brows arched in denial, and his mouth formed the word "oh" on a long, drawn-out breath. "I wouldn't do that, Laney." How could he tell her how he'd dreamed about her, how he watched her when she slept, how he thought about her every moment during the day? How could he tell her that she was already healing him, that his weakness for her was also proving to be his strength?

"Not deliberately," she said. Her eyes were still on the portrait, and he followed her gaze.

"Is it this house?" he asked finally. "Is it the pictures, the furniture, the things that were Patrice's?"

"Partially," she admitted with great effort. "I feel like everything I have really belongs to someone else."

His eyes made a careful study of the floor. Of course she'd feel that way. He'd practically rubbed it in her face. "Then we could go somewhere else. We could go to your house. Sort of . . . take it easy, watch TV, swim, maybe. Just the two of us."

Laney hesitated a moment. She'd never seen that warmth in anyone's eyes, at least not in connection with her. And that barrier

155

between them had given her an odd sense of security. She wasn't certain if she was ready to make herself vulnerable to another man.

Wes's eyes were longing, yearning, beseeching. His voice flowed over her racked nerves like warm, healing honey. "Please, Laney . . . I just want to get to know you better, without Amy looking over our shoulders."

She wanted to cry, not from pain or rejection but from rising joy. She wanted to be alone with him, too, wanted to finish that kiss. With a heavy sigh, she thought of the moments over the past few days when one smile from him, one touch, could have made all the difference in her world. If he offered it now, it could make all the difference in their marriage.

"All right," she whispered. "We'll go to my house."

Wes watched Laney from the kitchen window of her house as he stirred the iced tea he'd made. She stood beside the pool, her back to him, her hair sweeping across her back as the warm breeze flirted incessantly with it. The pool lights were on, bathing her in a blue, undulating light in the darkness. He closed his eyes and moaned. She was so beautiful it almost hurt to look at her.

She was still tense. Even now, looking at her from so far away, he could see the stress in her shoulders, in the way she balled her hands into fists, in the stiff set of her spine. He watched her dip a toe in the water as her skirt flapped across her calves, and realized there was more to her fear than the ghost of Patrice. Coming to this house hadn't changed things. It had only made her escape one set of threatening memories to face another. Maybe, he thought as he dropped the ice cubes into the glasses, she needed healing too.

She didn't hear him when he walked out to her, and quietly he put the glasses on the ground and lowered to the concrete beside her. When he reached out to take her hand and she gave it freely, he realized he'd been granted a second chance . . .

A second chance, Laney thought. He was giving her a second chance to love. A second chance to trust. But what if she failed again?

She had felt that warmth before, had been seduced beside this very pool, had made love in that house when her father was out of town. She had fallen in love, and it had been a mistake that changed her life.

Wes didn't demand anything of her. He only sat quietly beside her, staring out across the water.

"Laney." His voice was soft against the night. "Tell me about him," he said. "About Amy's father. He was the only one, wasn't he?"

"The first and the last," she whispered.

They were quiet for a moment, but Wes did not push her. His thumb made a light circular pattern on her hand, a simple gesture that spoke volumes, and she suddenly wanted him to know.

"I was eighteen when we met," she said softly. "He was nineteen."

"Were you in love with him?"

"Yes," she whispered. "Hopelessly."

A pine straw fell into the pool, and they watched it float across the surface. "He was a freshman at LSU, home for the summer, and I was just out of high school. He told me he loved me, said we'd get married. I believed him."

"What was he like?"

Tension seeped out of her with a slow exhalation of breath, and her head relaxed against his shoulder.

"He had sandy hair and blue eyes," she whispered. "He was in prelaw. Had aspirations of going into politics. He probably did. He was a lot like my father, I think. Hard to get to know, almost cold in his own way, and when you got some interest out of him, you felt like you'd accomplished something wonderful. But looking back, I see that it was part of his technique. I found out later I wasn't the only one he was seeing at the time."

"And you got pregnant."

"Yes," she whispered. "And when I told him that we would have to get married, he laughed at me. He wanted me to get an abortion. He said that I wasn't mature enough to be a mother and that he wouldn't let me trap him that way."

Wes's hand tightened.

"He went back to school after that, and I never saw him again. Just like that. He didn't know or care what I had done with the baby."

"What a fool," he whispered. The words, the declaration, hung inconclusively in the night air. Was he reacting as a father, a friend, or a lover? she wondered. Finally Wes said, "But I'm glad it happened."

"Why?"

"Because if it hadn't been for him, I wouldn't have wound up with Amy . . . or you."

She closed her eyes, resisting the urge to latch on to the illusion of something that wasn't hers. Could it be that he was falling in love with her? Could it be that she loved him? Could it be that this time that volatile emotion wouldn't break her heart?

He tucked her hair behind her ear. "You've been through so much. Are you happy now, Laney?"

She squeezed her eyes more tightly. "Yes," she whispered. "I'll never be Patrice. I know that, but—"

"You're different from Patrice," he cut in firmly. "But that's good. I need someone who's different. If you were the same, it would be harder . . ."

Harder to do what? she wanted to ask. To forget Patrice? To fall in love again? But those were questions she had no right to ask.

He looked over at her, and she would have given every cent she owned to know what he was thinking. "You really do make everything easy, Laney."

She couldn't meet his eyes, for she couldn't risk letting him see the hope rising in them.

"This all makes you uncomfortable, doesn't it, Laney?"

"What?" she asked, making herself look at him.

"Anything that borders on . . . intimate? You're afraid of me, aren't you?"

She tried to find an honest answer, for she wasn't certain herself. Keeping each other at arm's length was safe, but it didn't breed happiness. Yet the very thought of it growing into more left so much potential for heartache . . .

"I don't want either of us to be hurt," she whispered. "We've both had our share."

"And I don't want you to be uncomfortable," he said. "We don't have to sit here and keep wondering where this will lead. We could go to a movie, get some dinner, then go back home and sleep the way we've slept for the past few weeks. No pressure."

She couldn't hide the intense disappointment that fell over her, nor the intense relief. "OK," she said with a smile.

With the pressure gone, they went out like two people at the threshold of a relationship, getting to know each other on a date, and forgetting the marriage that stood like a wall between them.

Laney had expected her sense of well-being to be chased away when they arrived at Sherry's the next morning to pick up Amy.

But the child seemed to have lost all her hostility of the previous day, and she bubbled over with stories about the movie, the popcorn balls she and Sherry had made, and the fact that she'd gotten to stay up until eleven o'clock. Her stories were addressed as exuberantly to Laney as they were to Wes, and when she disappeared into the bedroom to get her overnight case, Sherry took Laney aside.

"Don't let her fool you. She spent most of the night with that little book you made for her. It was just what she needed, Laney."

Laney saw that Sherry was right as Amy babbled all the way home, laughing and giggling. But when she suddenly grew serious as they arrived home and asked them to sit down, Laney held her breath in fear.

"I was thinking," Amy said, as if she'd given it a great deal of thought, "that with school out soon and me being able to stay home with Laney every day, there isn't going to be that much to do. Wouldn't it be better if we lived at her house, where we could swim whenever we wanted, and I'd have that neat bedroom she fixed for me, and I could invite my friends over and . . ."

Laney's hand came up to cover her mouth, and she turned to Wes, eager to share her joy with him. But the blank look on his face changed everything.

"No. We're staying here. This is where we live."

"But, Daddy, this house is too small. Why should we live here when we have a big house we could live in?"

"Because it's our home," he said sternly. "Besides, Laney's house is for sale."

"I could take it off the market," Laney said quickly. Her eyes were pleading, entreating. "Wes, she wants to."

"I don't care," he said, standing up. His mouth trembled. "*I* don't want to."

"But, Daddy—"

"I don't want to discuss it anymore," he said. And before another argument could be uttered, he went back to the bedroom and closed the door.

Amy stood with her arms crossed, gaping at the closed door, and turned back to Laney. "I just thought it would be nice," she said, her lip quivering. "We don't *have* to."

Laney pulled Amy close and made her look into her eyes. "It's hard for him to leave here," she said quietly. "We have to give him more time."

"OK," Amy whispered with a dejected shrug. "I'll go put my stuff away."

Laney watched as Amy, her spirits suddenly lagging, vanished into her room. What happened? she wondered, astounded. How had she gone from the mountaintop to the barren valley? How had he given her such hope last night then turned his back on her this morning?

Quietly she slipped into the bedroom.

Wes was sitting on the bed, facing Patrice's picture, pain and confusion etched in the lines of his face. "I'm sorry," he said without looking at her.

"I know." She sat down next to him on the bed. "I know it's hard for you," she whispered, glancing at Patrice's picture. "But think of Amy, Wes. This is such a big step. It means she's accepting our marriage. Maybe she's even accepting me."

He didn't answer. His eyes remained locked on Patrice's face.

"She's ready to move on, to put the past behind her. It'll always be a part of her, just like your past will be a part of you. You can both take your past with you wherever you go. But Amy needs a clean break. She's torn, and she feels those memories tugging at her."

He nodded, saying without words that he understood that feeling for he felt it himself.

"It would be good to leave here," Laney whispered. "Amy doesn't want to slip me into the empty slot in her life that says 'mother.' By doing that she probably feels she'd be erasing Patrice completely. If we go to my house, start over in a new environment, she won't be covering the old memories with new ones. They could coexist."

He sighed heavily. Her wisdom wasn't just for Amy. It was for him too. He squeezed his eyes shut. "It's hard," he said.

"Of course it's hard," she said. "And I realize that one of the reasons we got married in the first place was so you could keep this house. But you were doing it for Amy—and now she wants to leave."

He got up and went to the dresser, braced his elbows on it, and hung his head.

"I can't afford the mortgage on your house, Laney. I still owe you all that money. I hate that. I can't stand the thought of living off you."

"But the house is paid for. And we're married, Wes. Everything I have is yours. I want it to be that way. My father's money never gave me one minute of happiness until I was able to share it with you."

Wes turned back around and regarded the beautiful woman sitting on his bed. Nothing in her generosity should have threatened him, yet it did. The fact that he had taken her money once haunted him daily whenever his own role as provider came to his mind.

"So much has changed," he moaned. "In the last year, our lives have turned upside down. This house has been the only thing that's stayed the same. It's just like it was when Patrice was alive. I need that."

The confession moved Laney, and she stood up and faced him. "I know you do, Wes. But the memories can go with you. You can pack them in boxes. You don't have to make Amy live in them."

He closed his eyes and pulled her into a fierce hug, and for a moment he rested his forehead on her crown. "It's hard to pack memories in boxes," he whispered.

"I know it is," she said. "But I'll help you. I'll help both of you."

He looked slowly around the room. If a real relationship with Laney was ever going to have the chance to develop, he would have to stop clinging to his guilt and his ghosts. Leaving would be like stepping out of the cloak that had been his life and stepping into a new one. It terrified him; it hurt him. But it was time he made a sacrifice for Laney. She had given him so much. And she'd never had a cloak of her own—not one that fit. It was so little for them to ask of him. And so much.

He tightened his embrace and set his forehead against hers, closing his eyes so she couldn't see his pain. "All right," he said at length. "We'll move. For you and Amy."

CHAPTER FIFTEEN

To make the move easier for all of them, Laney suggested that they pack only the things they would have immediate need for and come back for the rest as they needed it. That way, she reasoned, they could ease into the move without making it seem so final. Since Wes made no effort to sell his house, she knew it would be quite some time before he was ready to empty it completely of its memories.

The move, however, drew her closer to Amy and, surprisingly, to Patrice. As they sat on the floor and went through Amy's things, deciding what to leave and what to take, Laney found herself hurting for the woman who had been forced to leave it all behind.

"What's this?" she asked Amy when she found an old, threadbare doll with a stained face and only a trace of a mouth and eyes.

"It's the doll I used to carry around when I was a baby. Mommy made it for me."

Laney examined the doll. Despite the wear and tear, it had obviously been lovingly crafted. Smiling, she laid it aside and opened the little memory box that sat on a shelf. "Can I look in here?"

"Sure," Amy said, taking it from her hands and gazing through the contents. "It's my memory box. This is the ribbon I got for perfect attendance in choir at church. And this is the rose Mommy and Daddy got for me to wear to church one Easter. And this is the little Bible that Mommy gave me when I was baptized."

Laney looked down at her, her eyes misting over. "You were baptized? Already?"

"Brother Alan says I have a very mature understanding of salvation for my age. I was five then." She took the Bible out and feathered her fingertips across the lettering. "I'm really glad Mommy was still here when I got saved, so she knew for sure that I'd be with her someday. Daddy said God worked it all out that way." Amy looked up at her. "When were you baptized, Laney?"

Laney shook her head. "I wasn't."

"Never? Really?"

"My father didn't raise me in church. He didn't believe in anything he couldn't see."

Amy's eyes rounded as she gazed up at Laney. "But you believe, don't you?"

Laney gazed down at her daughter. "I didn't before. But I'm seeing God's work all around me now. Miracles. Yes, I believe."

"But have you asked Jesus into your heart?" The question came very natural to the child, and seemed very sweet, and it filled Laney with a deep sadness that something profound was lacking in her life.

"No, honey, I don't guess I ever have."

"But he'll come, if you'll ask him. I promise, Laney. It's the coolest thing. I can help you ask him, if you want me to."

Laney wasn't sure why tears assaulted her with such force, but her face twisted, and she covered her mouth. "Would you do that for me?"

Amy got on her knees and put her arms around Laney's neck. "I'll tell you what to say to him," she whispered.

And beginning with "Dear Jesus," Amy led Laney into the prayer of salvation.

When they were finished, Laney sobbed against her daughter's shoulder and clung to her with a mixture of joy and love and overwhelming gratitude.

"Now I'll have all of my family with me in heaven," Amy said. "You and Daddy and Mommy. Everybody I love."

That night, when Wes came home, he immediately noticed a change in Laney. She was calmer and smiled more, and he wondered if it had something to do with the move.

"So what did you guys do today?" he asked Amy while Laney was making supper.

With big, round eyes, Amy looked up at her father. "We talked about Jesus," Amy whispered. "And I helped Laney ask Jesus into her heart."

He caught his breath. "You . . . you did?"

"Yes, Daddy. She cried, and then she called Brother Alan, and he came over, and . . ."

Wes let her go and stood up, trying to determine how much of this was his child's imagination and how much was reality. "Are you telling me that Laney prayed?"

"With me, and then with Brother Alan. But don't tell her I told you. Let her do it. She needs to confess it before man, you know. I'm just a girl."

Tears came to his eyes, and he lifted his child up into his arms. "You are an amazing little angel, do you know that?"

"Why, Daddy?"

"Because . . ."

He stopped short when Laney breezed in with two bowls of vegetables in her hands. "Are you guys ready to eat?"

Wes swallowed and tried to look natural. "Sure. I'm starved."

She set the bowls down then looked up at Wes. A shy smile crept across her face. "Did Amy tell you what happened to me today?"

He set Amy down and met the child's eyes. She nodded that it was all right to tell. "Well, yes. She said that you'd made a profession of faith."

Laney smiled openly. "That sounds so cold. Not at all like what happened to me." She reached out for him, and Wes pulled her into his arms and crushed her.

"I'm so happy for you, Laney."

"I'm getting baptized Sunday, Wes. I hope that's not a bad time."

He pulled back to look at her, laughing with joy. "A bad time? Are you kidding?"

And as he held her, he recommitted his own life to the One who had taken a lie and turned it into truth.

That night, Laney and Amy went back into the child's room to resume their packing. Looking around the room, she saw it with new eyes. Eyes that didn't count the loss but saw only the gain. Eyes that didn't recall the darkness but saw only the light.

And there was light in Patrice's legacy to her daughter. Beautiful light in the ceramic clowns that Patrice had painted, lattice hangings, quilted dolls. They hadn't had much money, but Patrice had made them wealthy in other ways. "We'll take all of this," she whispered finally. "They belong with you."

She found herself wishing she had met the woman when she began helping Wes pack. She saw Patrice's sense of humor in the silly gifts she had bought for him: a huge polka-dot bow tie that she'd given him for a birthday, a pair of size fifty-four boxing shorts with hearts all over them, plaid socks, a Scottish kilt.

Wes caught her gazing with a smile on her face at the woman's portrait beside the bed, and he stopped folding the clothes he was stacking into a box.

"I think I would have liked her," Laney said finally.

Moved again, Wes gazed with her at the picture. "I think she would have liked you," he whispered.

She looked up at him, expecting him to still be gazing at the picture, but his eyes were on her, instead. Her heart caught at his yearning expression. "You just don't know what you do to me, Laney."

Hope rose to block her throat. She touched his stubbled jaw with disbelieving fingers. "Tell me."

He moved her hand to his mouth and held it there as his brows came together. "You make me forget the pain, but you create a new pain."

She stared up at him. A new pain. He felt it, too. "Then why?" she asked. "Why have you avoided me? Why have you been coming home late, working weekends—"

"Because being near you drives me crazy," he said simply. "Because I can't really even touch you, and I want to. But wanting to seems like such a betrayal . . . it doesn't make sense, I know, but it's there."

"It's OK," she whispered.

She caught her breath as his lips came down on hers with the gentleness of a sigh, cleansing her of her fears and phantoms, bathing her in warmth and hope. He was almost husband, almost lover, almost friend.

After a moment, he broke the kiss and gazed down at her, touching her face as if she were a precious treasure. "I was thinking, Laney . . . about all the guilt I've felt. About our marriage. The way we did it."

It was clear something was missing, but she wasn't sure what he meant.

Recognizing her confusion, he met her eyes as his grew misty. "It never feels good to go against God's will. It always makes me miserable."

"And you think our marriage was against his will?"

He thought for a moment. "It might have been in his will, eventually, but we didn't give him time. And because we rushed so, we deprived ourselves of the opportunity to get to know each other. To get closer. Maybe even to fall in love."

She didn't know what to say, so she only gazed up at him, waiting for whatever he was leading to.

"But it's so funny how God always makes provisions for our mistakes. He works around them, you know? Uses them."

He stared at her for a long moment, and it was clear that this wasn't easy for him.

"He's making me fall in love with you, anyway," he said. "It's the craziest thing. And now we're equally yoked. There's really no reason . . ."

She caught her breath as he kissed her again.

"Laney," he whispered against her lips, "would you consider setting things right?"

"How?" she whispered.

He combed his fingers through the back of her hair and pressed his forehead against hers. "Would you consider marrying me again? This time for real? In the church, with God blessing us?"

Slowly, she stood straighter and gazed at him with astonishment. "You want to marry me again?"

"Yes," he whispered. "Right now, I don't know whether to go forward or backward. I feel like I'm cheating if I get close to you, like the Devil's got some terrible hold on me, and he's using my past and my own marriage against me. I want it to be real, Laney, so I can act on my feelings. So I can be happy about falling in love with you, rather than miserable."

She breathed in a sob and covered her mouth. Would a real marriage keep the memories of Patrice out? Would it help him to forget and cleave to her?

Maybe, she thought. And if not, she would be patient. All she wanted now was to be Wes's wife—in more than name. "Yes . . . I'll . . . I'll marry you again . . ."

"Tonight?" he whispered. "We'll get Sherry to watch Amy, and we'll go talk to Alan and get him to do it all over, right there in the church."

"Tonight," she whispered, teetering between laughter and tears.

Alan came over from the parsonage at nine and met them in his office, wearing a pair of jeans and a sweatshirt. "What's going on?" he asked.

Wes reached for Laney's hand and squeezed it. "We want you to marry us, Alan."

Alan frowned and leaned forward. "Didn't we already do that?"

"Yeah, we did. But I wasn't being honest with you. And I wasn't being honest with God."

Alan's eyebrows lifted, and smiling, he leaned back in his chair.

"Now, I want to make a real commitment. Under God. I want him to be at the center of this covenant."

Alan smiled at the tears in Laney's eyes. "And how do you feel about this, Laney?"

Laney was quiet for a moment, then finally, she tried to speak. "Everything changed for me today," she whispered. "I don't deserve any of this, but here it is. I don't know why he would bless me with my little girl and such a wonderful man after all the things I've done in my life . . ." Her voice broke off, but she tried to go on. "The fact that Wes wants to marry me again, for real, is just too good to be true. But if God could give me a gift like he gave me today, then he could give me this."

Alan looked down at his hands, his own eyes misty. "You don't know how I've been praying for this."

Laney looked surprised. "You have?"

"Ever since I performed your ceremony," he said. "I've felt so guilty. I shouldn't have done it, and I've asked God to forgive me and make your marriage a real one. I guess he just answered my prayer." He slapped his knees and grinned as he got to his feet. "All right, then. Let's go to the sanctuary and talk to God together."

They felt as giddy as teenagers as they headed for the sanctuary. Halfway up the hall, they saw Herman, the janitor, and his wife, Ruby, waxing the floor in the nursery.

"Hey, Herman!" Wes called, and the old man peeked out the door. "Want to be a witness at a wedding?"

Herman looked puzzled and stepped out into the hall, still holding his mop. His wife came out behind him.

"Wes?" she asked. "Who's getting married?"

"We are!" Wes said. "Come on. You can stand up for us."

"But . . . we're not dressed for it!"

"Neither are we!" Wes said.

Herman leaned the mop against the wall and loped toward them. "Thought you two already got married," he said.

"That's right," Ruby said. "I know Eugenia told us you'd already gotten married. She was a little miffed that she wasn't invited."

"Well, she'll be doubly miffed when she finds out we did it twice and left her out both times! You just tell her that I liked my new wife so much I decided to marry her twice!"

Laney laughed and fell against Wes.

When Herman reached them, he looked at Alan. "All this OK with you, Pastor?"

Alan grinned. "I'm game if you are."

Herman looked them both over, then let a tiny grin crack through his usually bland features. "Well, all right. Ruby, it looks like we're going to a wedding."

"Beats mopping the floor," Ruby said on a high-pitched laugh.

They went into the small sanctuary and gathered at the altar, and suddenly all the laughter faded and the giddy smiles settled into serene ones. The Holy Spirit was with them.

Alan's voice was reverent, soft, as he spoke.

"Tonight, when I saw the joy on both of your faces and felt the thrill you both felt at the idea of doing it before God, asking for his blessings, I couldn't help feeling that it was all in his plan. I'm honored to be here with you as you commit your lives to each other under God." He swallowed back the emotion cracking his voice, and said, "Wes, do you take Laney as your lawfully wedded wife?"

Wes listened to the vows this time, savoring every one, seriously looking forward to fulfilling each one with her. "I do," he said.

"And Laney, do you take Wes to be your lawfully wedded husband?"

Tears came to her eyes as the vows were repeated, sweetly, seriously, with a different spirit this time. This time, she hadn't coerced him. This time, it was his idea. It wasn't money that was the catalyst or Amy or any number of other things. It was love. Even though he hadn't said it outright, in so many words, she thought he was beginning to love her. Not as much as Patrice, perhaps, but she would take whatever he gave her.

"Laney and Wes, by the power vested in me by God and the state of Louisiana, I hereby pronounce you husband and wife."

Wes leaned down and kissed her hard, deep, with all the passion that he'd held back since the first time he'd tasted her. The kiss lingered on, and her fear vaporized like a fog in a cool, dry wind. He was her husband, she thought. Her real husband. And he took pleasure in her kiss, her touch . . . Tonight, he would take pleasure in her body.

Alan cleared his throat, but the kiss didn't break. "You may kiss the bride," he teased softly. The janitor and his wife began to laugh, and finally, Wes pulled his lips away from Laney's. Touching her face with his hand, he said, "Sorry, guys. But if you knew how badly I wanted to do that . . ."

Laney blinked back the tears in her eyes and turned to hug Ruby. "Thank you for being our witnesses."

"It's not like you needed us," Ruby said, hugging her back. "There's nothing to sign. You're already married."

"You were needed," Wes said. "You were needed so you could tell everyone who asks that Wes is elated with his new wife. That our marriage is not a sham."

"I'll call Eugenia first thing in the morning," Ruby laughed, clapping her hands together. "Now, you two go home and start your lives together. Again."

Laney reached out to hug Alan. He had given her a cursory hug at the first wedding, but she'd felt his reluctance to hold out too much hope for either of them. This time, however, his hug spoke volumes. "God has funny ways of working," he said. "I'm always amazed, but I'm never surprised."

Feeling as if she would burst with joy and excitement and gratitude, Laney let Wes pull her out of the church and back to the car.

She was nervous as they drove home. Their first wedding night had been filled with uncertainty, but there was no uncertainty now. She knew where tonight would lead them, and she felt an almost childish excitement about it. Yet it still frightened her. The one time she had been with a man had turned out badly. Now she didn't really know what he expected from her, what he needed, how he wanted her to behave.

He seemed to grow quieter as they grew closer to his house, and she began to wonder if he regretted what had happened. When he pulled into his driveway, he left the car idling but made no move to get out.

"What's wrong?" she whispered.

He started to speak, stopped, then tried again. "I want this to be right," he whispered. "Perfect. You deserve that."

"It will be," she whispered.

"Would it . . . would it bother you if we had our honeymoon at your house?" he asked. "I mean, I know we haven't moved in over there yet, but it is going to be our home together, and it just makes more sense."

Her heart sank. She knew the real reason he didn't want to share their honeymoon night here. Already Patrice's memory had come between them.

He seemed to read her thoughts and leaning across the seat, slid his fingers through her hair. His lips brushed hers, chaste but promising. "Don't look so crestfallen," he whispered. "It's you I want to be with. Without distractions."

"I want that, too," she whispered. "My house is fine if you don't feel comfortable here."

He kissed her, then backed the car out and headed back across town.

Laney tried not to let herself dwell on his preoccupation with Patrice, though she knew he didn't want to take her home and make love to her on the bed he'd shared with his first wife. He wanted to do it someplace else, almost in secret, so that Laney wouldn't taint Patrice's memory.

They reached Laney's house, and she found herself uncertain again as they went to the door.

"Wait a minute," Wes said, taking the key from her hand and unlocking the door himself. He smiled down at her, lifted her in his arms, and carried her over the threshold. "Welcome home, Mrs. Grayson."

Her fears and worries about Patrice and why he had brought her here vanished as her feet touched the ground again, and Wes drew her closer. He kissed her, deeper than he had at the church, and she felt the hunger that had been hidden away since the first night she had shared a bedroom with him. Her anxieties melted away one by one as the new freedom of her marriage released her.

"That apricot scent," he whispered. "It's driven me crazy since the first day I met you."

She couldn't answer. Her voice was lost somewhere in the electricity his words sparked.

"I've watched you sleep sometimes at night, Laney," he went on. "And I've fought myself to keep from slipping under the covers next to you . . . holding you . . ."

She slid her arms around his neck with a freedom she hadn't known before and sought his lips again. He kissed her with a ravenous urgency, creating the same urgency in her.

When her knees seemed weak and her hands trembled, he lifted her again and carried her up the stairs.

Amazed at the miracle of this newfound love and the sweetness of their covenant together, they cherished each other without inhibition, then slept for the first time as man and wife.

After her baptism on Sunday night, they spent their first night as a family in Laney's house. Amy had fallen asleep on the couch after supper, exhausted from the day's move, and had been carried to her new bed. Laney wanted to be alone with Wes, to tell him she loved him, to hear him say he loved her. She wanted to hear him say that he trusted her completely, enough to combine checking accounts and stop trying to pay her back for every penny she spent on him . . . and every cent she had given him. But one dream at a time was the most she hoped for, and having her new family opening up to her for the first time seemed so much already.

She tried to leave Wes alone as he lay on the daybed beside the glass doors looking out over the pool. His pensive, distant mood probably shouldn't be disturbed, she decided. So she made herself busy cleaning the kitchen then putting away some of the toys Amy had left in the den. She tried to move quietly, feeling she wasn't welcome in his thoughts, feeling that, perhaps, he regretted everything that had happened over the past few days. Maybe he felt he had given her too much of himself, and by doing so had taken too much from Patrice. Laney struggled to understand, to be stoic, to be patient.

But when he reached out and pulled her down beside him as she was tiptoeing by, the relief and gratitude washing over her told her she was as weak as a dandelion puff where he was concerned.

"Why are you being so quiet?" he asked.

"Because you are."

"I'm sorry," he said. "There's just so much on my mind. So much has happened so fast."

"I know. Too fast, maybe."

He gave her a considering look. "You think so?"

"Don't you?"

"I don't know."

They looked at the pool, at the blue lights dancing as the wind rippled over the surface.

"Maybe I've pushed this family thing a little too hard," Laney said after a while. "I could let up if you want me to. I could even sleep in another room if you want . . . if you want to be alone tonight. I know it's hard for you."

"Is that what you want?" he asked. "To sleep in another room?"

She sighed wearily. "What do you want, Wes? I just want what you want."

His arm moved around her waist and he nuzzled his mouth into her hair. "I just want to be close to you."

She closed her eyes and drew a deep breath. It was happening, she thought. Dreams were coming true. "I want that too," she whispered. They sat like that for a segment of eternity, unmoving, until Laney whispered, "I was so afraid."

"Afraid of what?"

"Of liking Patrice. Of knowing what a good person she was. What a loss she was to you and Amy. I was afraid I'd see how inadequate I am in comparison. How lacking—"

He turned on his side and hushed her with the tips of his fingers. "You aren't lacking in anything," he whispered. "And I don't compare you to Patrice. You're different."

"I don't blame you," she assured him. "You can't help but compare us. And it isn't your fault."

"Laney, look at you," he whispered. "You're an angel in a pair of cutoff shorts. You're a black-haired Godiva, a beautiful Florence Nightingale. You're a breath of fresh air. Why would I want to compare you to anyone when you're so much already?"

She looked at him with astounded black eyes. Did he really see her that way? Not as someone who had forced her way into his life with the threat of taking his daughter? Not as someone who wanted more and more each time she looked at him? Did he really see what she *gave* instead?

She loved him, she thought as he kissed her. She loved him so much her heart was breaking. And she knew that he was beginning

174

to love her. For now, she would take as little or as much as he offered for as long as he offered it.

It was after midnight when the warmth surrounding Laney was removed and she woke to a cold, empty bed. Slowly, she rose and slipped into her robe. A movement outside near the pool caught her eye, and she went to the glass doors in her bedroom and looked out.

She saw Wes's silhouette on the end of a chaise lounge. He was staring into the pool, elbows propped on his knees. His shoulders were slumped dejectedly, and a deep sigh made his back rise and fall.

Was he thinking about Patrice again?

As despair filled her heart, she recalled the comfort and the peace she had felt with him the night they had prayed together and renewed their vows and sought that peace and comfort again. "Help him to let go of Patrice, Lord," she whispered. "Help me to help him." Tears ran over her cheeks, and she pressed her forehead against the cool glass. "I love him."

She saw him stir, as if he was getting ready to come back in, and she crawled back into bed. How much time would it take to pull him through that elusive door between past and future? Or would it ever happen? Would she wake one day to find that the love he'd shown her had only been illusion, his illusion that she was someone else?

Wes had said he would never do that, but what kind of choices did people really have in matters of their hearts? She heard the door slide open, felt him crawling in beside her, heard him expel a weary breath as he settled next to her.

And then, as if it was the most natural gesture in the world, he curled around the bend of her body and set his arm over her waist. In a moment she felt him drift off to sleep, holding her as if he loved her, embracing her as if there was no one between them.

A month of loving nights crept by, a month of insecure days. Wes still didn't put his house on the market, and Laney saw his thoughts drifting off into the distance when he thought she didn't see. She still felt Patrice's ghost keeping their scarred souls from joining.

But Amy was happy. She was learning to sew and to dive and was developing a tan that bespoke her heritage. When she fell off her bike she went to Laney. When she fought with her friends she went to Laney. When she needed to talk about Patrice she went to Laney.

Laney kept her mind off of her worries about Wes by staying busy. Determined to make this house their home rather than her father's, she set about cleaning out an accumulation of thirty years. She sat on the floor in the study one July afternoon, sifting through the stacks of papers and notebooks her father had stacked in a closet.

"Laney, the thread ran out."

Amy stood in the doorway, the picture of American youth in her braids and bare feet, her bathing suit covered by only a pair of shorts. In her hands was the shirt that Laney had labored over for Wes's birthday, her first attempt at men's clothes since she had bought her sewing machine. Sherry had helped her with some of the basics in the beginning, then taught her a few tricks to make the job easier. Amy's job was to do all the basting and hem the shirt, and Laney had even allowed her to use the machine for a few practice pieces under close supervision.

"Bring me the spool," Laney said, not getting up. She broke the thread and directed it through the needle. "You're doing a good job. Your dad will think we bought this."

"He's gonna be surprised," Amy said. "Maybe he'll wear it when we take him out that night."

"Of course he will." A soft smile of anticipation stole across her lips. Hopefully, Wes would be proud enough of the shirt that he wouldn't notice the wobbly stitches or the flaws in the construction. It was, after all, the thought that counted. Besides, the sleeves were exactly the same length. It had taken her three tries, but she was certain they were perfect now.

Amy curled her tongue over her lips and jabbed the needle back in the hem.

"Take it back in there, honey," Laney ordered. "The light's too dim in here."

Without looking up, Amy wandered back into the den.

Laney dusted off the manuscript box in her hand and opened it. Her father had been notorious for never throwing anything away. Every draft of every manuscript he'd ever written, from notes about ideas to the final draft, was kept in that closet. She recalled the reporters who had gathered in the house when he had won awards for his work, taking pictures of drafts of manuscripts stacked ceiling-high. And she remembered how he had taken more pleasure in that media attention than he had in his own daughter.

She lifted off the top page and glanced at the second. It was a letter of some sort, scrawled in ink and yellow with age. She sifted through the pages for the first page and found that it had been written to her mother.

A frown marred her forehead, and she dug through the stack and found that the box was full of letters to her mother. Several were written before their marriage. Some were written during it. And one . . . one was written after her mother's death.

Laney rose from the floor and went to the rocking chair beside the window, where the light was better. The early letters were written by a young man in love with an Indian girl. He wrote about the disdain of her people and his, about the burning passion that he declared would not be snuffed by bigotry and discrimination.

Laney found the letters her mother wrote in answer, that she would forsake the wishes of the people on her reservation and run away with him if it was the only way they could be together. She read of her mother's love for her parents, of her wish to someday return to the Caddo reservation in Arkansas and make things better for them, but that, for now, she had to follow her heart and be with the man she loved. It would mean, perhaps, that her parents would turn their backs on her for good, but for him it was worth it.

Her father told her that he, too, would be looked down on for crossing racial barriers. But he declared, in the rich, lyrical style that had made him famous, that he would rather live as an outcast with her for the rest of his life than be accepted in a world without her for a single day.

Laney swallowed the emotion swelling in her throat. Had he really loved? Had he really been able? She read on through the years of their marriage, through the changes that took place in his fame and his success. She read of their joy over the birth of a daughter, letters written in his absence when he was away researching his masterpiece. And through it all, their love was sustained.

And then . . .

Laney barely remembered her mother's death. But what weighed heavily in her mind was her father's anger, his coldness, his bitterness after that. She came to the last letter. It was dated five years after her mother's death, when Laney was fourteen.

Laney wept as she read the laments of a man who had never been able to say good-bye to his wife, a man who blamed himself for not being able to die in her place, a man who wouldn't allow himself the luxury of love again for as long as he lived. She read of his despair over seeing his wife each time he looked at his daughter, of his inability to ever reach out again.

She set the letters down and let her eyes roam over the hundreds of books lining the walls of his study. One shelf was devoted to his own writings. She recalled the critics' acclaim about his work after her mother's death. They had praised the "tragic voice," the "mood of one crying out in agony," the "passion unfulfilled." He was growing wiser with age, they had said.

But now Laney knew he was only growing lonelier.

She returned the letters to their box and put it back in the closet.

What did it all mean? That he would have loved her if he'd been able? That there was a reason for his coldness, and it had nothing to do with her own failure as his child? That he had never been able to forget the woman he had loved and lost?

She sat on the desk and closed her eyes, dropping her forehead into her palm. She had spent a lifetime competing, against her will, with the ghost of one woman. Now she found herself competing with another. Was it her destiny to love and want to please men who clung to memories with more fervor than they clung to her?

"What's the matter, Laney?" Amy stood in the doorway, her innocent face full of concern at Laney's expression.

Laney opened her arms. "Come here," she whispered.

Amy didn't hesitate, and her tight hug made things infinitely better.

"I was just looking through my dad's things," she explained. "And understanding him a little."

Amy looked up at her. "Then you aren't mad at him anymore?"

Laney bit her lip and looked at the old cardboard box. "No, Amy. I'm not mad anymore. Just a little sad, that's all."

She held her daughter against her, accepting the love the child was offering and praying that she had the strength to see the blessings she had rather than the things that would forever be kept from her.

CHAPTER SIXTEEN

Wes drove home from work a week later with a smile on his face. It was his birthday, and Amy and Laney had been up to something for the past three weeks. He had no idea what it was. He was only aware of the mad dash to hide the evidence of whatever they were doing each time he came home early, and the conspiratorial giggles and secretive winks across the table whenever they pretended they didn't know his birthday was coming. Even that morning they had avoided mentioning what day it was, but their discretion had been blatantly obvious.

He pulled his car into the long driveway and sighed. It felt good to be happy again, to look forward to going home to his family. His family, he thought. It *was* becoming a family in many, many ways. And he found himself thinking about Patrice less and less as his love for Laney grew.

He tapped the wallet in his back pocket and smiled at how good it had felt to write the enormous check folded there. It would free him—free them both—to love and move ahead without past superficial reasons hanging over them. It would take away any thoughts that their marriage had been a neat little bargain. If things were ever going to move from "yours" and "mine" to "ours," he had to clear the debt he felt hanging over him like a cloud. It meant nothing to her, he thought. But it meant a great deal to him. From now on there would only be the present and the bright, beckoning future.

He slammed the door to warn them he was home, then slipped into the house through the garage. Dimness and quiet greeted him. "Anybody home?" he asked.

Suddenly his wife and daughter leapt out at him, a roomful of balloons at their backs, and shouted, "Surprise!"

The three-member birthday party was a delight, and Wes couldn't remember the last time he'd laughed as hard as he did when Laney and Amy performed a mimed Amy Grant number, complete with choreography. When it came time to open presents, he oohed and ahhed over every item, gauging their faces to see if he had reached the one that was so special to them. And when he finally got to the shirt that had been so lovingly stitched by both his women, he was moved to silence.

"Don't you like it, Daddy?" Amy asked anxiously.

He seemed to struggle with a knot in his throat. "It's beautiful. No one's ever made me a shirt before." He drew in a deep sigh and brought effervescent eyes up to Laney. "So this is what you two have been up to."

Amy beamed, and Laney dipped her head, suddenly unable to meet his eyes.

Amy pointed to one of the crooked seams. "I did this part on the machine, and I hand-stitched the hem and some of the embroidery."

"Embroidery?"

Amy snatched the shirt from his hand and turned up the collar. "See? Right here. It says, 'We love you.'"

Dark eyes collided with jade ones. A pink blush was climbing into Laney's cheeks, and her smile was faint, uncertain.

"It's the best present I've ever gotten," he said directly to her.

Laney gazed at him for a long moment, a tiny fissure of doubt drawing her brows together.

"And we're taking you out to eat, so go put it on," Amy ordered.

Wes wrenched his eyes from Laney and hopped to attention. "Yes, ma'am. I'll be the best-dressed man there. Just give me ten minutes."

He grabbed Laney by the waist and drew her gently against him. "And how about helping me, Mrs. Grayson?"

Laney kissed his chin. He wasn't withdrawing, as she'd dreaded after the declaration on his collar. Instead, he was kissing her temple, her eyelids, the tip of her nose.

Amy stayed behind as Laney followed him. When she had closed the door, he pulled her into his arms again. "You're special, you know that?" The gravelly emotion in his voice spread through her heart.

She set her fingertips over his lips. "So are you."

He moved her fingers and his lips touched hers, and she felt her heart mixing with his, all the pain and ache mingling with the joy and flutter of love. The kiss was different than their past kisses. It was more at home with her, more content in her touch, more secure in the permanency of her warmth.

He pulled back and let her go. "Did you and Amy really make this?" he asked, sliding his arms into the sleeves.

She fought the pride in her smile. "Yes. It isn't perfect, but—"

"Isn't perfect?" he cut in. "How can you say that? It's better than perfect! I didn't even know you could sew, much less that you were teaching Amy."

Her laughter rolled out easily. "Sherry taught me. Then when I got stumped, Amy and I put our heads together, and between us we figured out what we were doing."

He buttoned the shirt and stepped to the mirror to assess the fit. "That's why this family is working," he said softly. "When we get stumped we put our heads together and figure out what we're doing."

Laney stepped up behind him, carefully watching his reflection. "*Is* it working?" she asked hesitantly.

He turned around and framed her face, pressing his forehead against hers. "Of course it's working," he said. "And don't you forget it." They came together, and his kiss was shattering, straining the boundaries of sweet gentleness. After a moment, he pulled back. "Amy's waiting," he whispered on a note of regret.

"Yes," she whispered. He began tucking in his shirt. The wallet on his hip reminded him of the check, and he slipped it out. "I almost forgot," he said before she stepped away. "I have something for you too."

Laney's eyes twinkled as she smiled at him. "You got me something for your birthday?"

"Sort of," he said. His eyes sparkled with pride. "It's something that's been hanging over my head since we got married. Something that I've just now been able to settle."

"What?"

He looked down at his wallet then back at her. "I got the first payment today on the amusement park contract. It was enough to pay back the money you gave me."

She caught her breath and her expression fell as he pulled the check out of his billfold. He handed it to her, and she stepped back as if he was handing her a cup of poison.

"Wes, I really, really didn't expect to be paid back. Keep that money. Invest it in your business."

"Laney, one of the reasons I agreed to marry you was because of this money. Do you know how that makes me feel?"

"How?" she asked.

"Cheap," he said. "I want to make my own way, and I don't need your money to do it."

Laney's mouth trembled. "I make you feel cheap?"

"No!" he said. "I didn't mean that."

She caught her breath and forced herself to stay calm. "All right, I should have seen that. I even deserve it."

"Laney . . ." He reached out to touch her, but she recoiled, gripping her arms around her waist as if it was the only embrace in her destiny.

"Give me the check if it makes you feel better," she said. "I never meant to make you feel like I owned you. I thought we had built something here."

"Laney, we have. You don't understand. You're misinterp—"

"No, Wes, I do understand. And really . . . it's fine. If you want to pay me back . . ." But her tears belied her words as her voice trailed off.

Confused, Wes handed her the check. "Laney, I didn't do this to hurt you. I only wanted to be able to go on with our marriage without—"

"I know," she interrupted, smearing her tears across her face. "Please hurry and get ready," she choked on her way to the door. "Amy's waiting for us."

The rest of Wes's birthday was a lesson in civility, an exercise in spurious enjoyment despite the disappointment and hurt swirling just beneath the surface. Laney's only comments were directed at Amy, and her eyes held a fragile, shattered quality that he felt was unwarranted. What did she think? That by paying her back he was cutting himself off from her? Did she think all the love and tenderness and passion they had shared had been an act? Did she really think he was only doing what he'd been hired to do?

It made him furious when she avoided meeting his eyes as he helped her and Amy back into the car after dinner. It was as if she had just been waiting for some reason to doubt him, he thought, some reason to prove that life would continue to cheat her of what she held dear.

He drove home, maintaining a light conversation with his daughter, noting the way Laney gazed out the window as if everything she believed in had been snatched out from under her. Couldn't she see that he loved her, that he didn't want money to be any part of their reason for being together, that he needed to support her and care for her on his own? Didn't she see how good it made him feel to be able to give that money back?

She went to bed when Amy did, leaving him to hash the facts out in his mind. Where had he gone wrong? he asked himself. Had it been a mistake to love again, in spite of the prospect of someday losing that love? Had it been a mistake to reach out, knowing that reaching out could mean realizing how empty his life could be? Had it been a mistake to rejoice at what he'd believed was her love for him, when rejoicing quite possibly meant the deepest sadness a man could know?

The night grew older and he grew wiser as the pain in her eyes etched itself on his heart. None of those had been a mistake. But the check . . . the check had been his undoing.

He closed his eyes as he realized that, in her mind, paying her back had reduced their love to mere services rendered. Why hadn't he seen it before? Why hadn't he expected it? He pinched the bridge of his nose. She thought she was his albatross. She thought his feelings for her were borrowed, grudging, duty-bound, the way her father's had been.

He was bone tired by the time he went to the bedroom and found her lost in a deep slumber like a child whose only refuge was sleep. He'd been such a fool, he thought. He'd fostered her fears, nurtured her insecurities. Making her sleep for weeks under the portrait of

Patrice, clinging to the house like a kid would cling to a tattered blanket, holding on to yesterday when all he wanted to do was let go.

A deeper love than he had ever known for a woman filled him, and he crawled into bed next to her and slid his arms around her. She had been sleeping more and more lately, lying in bed longer than she should each morning, retiring earlier. Was it because she had been depressed? Had he been so thankful of his own happiness that he had overlooked hers?

He dropped a kiss on her temple and pulled her tighter against him. "I love you, Laney," he whispered, though she did not hear. "And tomorrow I'll prove it to you."

It was time to move forward, he told himself finally. It was time to say good-bye to Patrice, sell the house, and put his past where it belonged—in his heart and mind for the times when he needed it, but not in some tangible structure that had so little bearing on the present. His life with Laney was more than any man could want. And he had new castles to build with her.

Laney felt as if she'd been turned upside down and shaken when she woke the next morning. She had never had a hangover, but she had a strong suspicion that she might prefer it to the dizzy, nauseous, weak feeling gripping her. Wes was beside her, fully awake, watching the way she clutched her head and lay back down after starting to get out of bed. "I think I'm sick," she whispered.

He propped himself on an elbow and laid his hand on her forehead. "No fever," he said, his brows knitted. "Maybe it's a virus."

She closed her eyes and tried to lie still until her dizziness subsided. "Wes, I'm sorry. I was awful last night."

"It's OK," he said. "I understand why you thought what you did. But Laney, our marriage is still a marriage, now more than ever. I don't want that money to come between us somewhere down the road. By giving it back to you, I can feel free of that artificial bond we had in the beginning. And we can concentrate on the really important things."

"It's just that . . . it's just that we're on such shaky ground. I have trouble knowing what's really mine."

"I'm yours," he whispered. "Trust me."

She reached up to slide her arms around his neck, but queasiness assaulted her again and she dropped her head back down. Her skin was pallid and clammy, and her hands trembled.

As if he'd seen enough, Wes rolled over to the telephone, his motions abrupt and determined.

"Who are you calling?"

"The doctor," he said. "You're sick."

"But I don't have a doctor."

"Then it's time you got one," he said as he riffled through the phone book they kept in the nightstand drawer. "I'll call mine. He's the nicest man you'd ever want to meet, and he's become a good friend over the years."

"I'll be all right." She sat up and waited for her balance. "I think I'm feeling better already."

Wes ignored her. Within seconds he was making her an appointment for that morning. When he hung up, Laney forced herself to stand. "Wes, I really don't have to go to the doctor. See? I'm fine."

Wes got out of bed and pulled on his robe. "Laney, you've been unusually tired lately. There's obviously something wrong this morning. I don't believe in taking chances."

Of course he didn't, she thought with a sweet surge of warmth that made her feel even more ashamed of her actions last night. He'd seen firsthand what illness could do, and she'd do anything to lay his fears to rest. "OK, I'll go if it'll make you feel better."

He kissed her. "It will. Amy can come to the office with me and stay with Sherry while you're gone."

Laney wondered how she could have imagined that his offering the money back meant something less than a gesture of love. Even if her first conclusion had been sound, he continued to offer her more love than she had ever known. She got dressed, feeling better as the morning went on.

The doctor's office was decorated in a blend of burgundy and gray, lending a peaceful, secure feeling to the patients who waited. The wait wasn't long, however, and the doctor proved to be worth the trouble. He seemed to know all about her relationship to Amy and her marriage to Wes, and he welcomed her warmly, shaking her hand and smiling.

After half an hour of questions that he posed as idle chitchat, he took her symptoms and examined her, then left her with a smug smile on his face. In a few minutes he came back, his smile broader than before.

"What is it, Doctor? A virus?" she asked.

He chuckled and looked down at her chart. "Not quite. Something a little more serious, I think."

Her face went pale, and his laugh grew more boisterous. "It's a baby, Laney," he said. "You're going to have a baby."

"A what?"

"A baby," the doctor repeated.

Laney caught her breath. "But that's impossible. Wes is sterile. Amy was adopted."

The doctor leaned forward and patted her knee. The gentle smile on his leathered face bordered on amusement. "No, Laney. You've got it all wrong. It was Patrice who couldn't conceive, not Wes."

Dizziness crept over her again, and the air suddenly seemed thin. She touched her head, as if doing so could help her absorb this new development. A hesitant smile tugged at the corners of her lips. "Are you telling me that I'm going to have Wes's baby?"

The doctor patted her shoulder, and his voice was colored with genuine fondness. "Some things take a while to sink in, don't they, Laney? Yes, you're going to have Wes's baby. Would you like me to call him?"

She snapped out of her daze and let a silly smile take full control of her face. "No. No, I want to tell him. It can be a late birthday present." She covered her mouth. "Oh, Doctor," she whispered, "are you absolutely sure?"

He laughed again. "Absolutely."

Laney drove around for a while after she left the doctor's office. She was anxious to share the news with Wes—news that, she hoped, would cement things even further between them—but she wanted to be alone with the idea first. Was she really going to have the chance to rejoice in a pregnancy? Was she really going to take her baby home and nurse it and change its diapers and watch it grow? Was she really going to share her joy with the baby's father and sister?

"A baby," she said aloud. "I'm going to have a baby."

She drove to a maternity store and bought two dresses that wouldn't fit her for weeks. Then she went next door to the baby shop and bought a christening gown and a pacifier. Her baby, she thought over and over as she pressed her hand to her stomach with gentle reverence. Wes's baby.

Most of the morning had passed when she recalled the boxes of baby clothes that had belonged to Amy, boxes she had left in Amy's closet when they'd moved. She wondered now if her baby could wear any of them. There were blankets and little hats and tiny little socks. A flutter of excitement whirled inside her, and she headed for Wes's old house to find the box.

Her excitement waned, however, when she pulled into the driveway of the tiny house and saw Wes's truck. He was supposed to be at work, she thought. What was he doing?

Pressing her hand on her stomach, Laney quietly turned the knob and opened the door. Wes wasn't in the living room, so she stepped inside, careful to close the door soundlessly behind her.

She stood still for a moment, listening for the sound of a hammer repairing something she hadn't known was broken or the sound of boxes being moved out of the attic. Maybe he'd come to find some tool he needed at work, she told herself. But there was no sound. The house was dead quiet.

She wasn't sure why she stayed quiet as she moved toward the kitchen and glanced inside to see if he was there. But it had something to do with her feeling like an intruder, as if he'd made this date with his past, and she hadn't been invited.

When he wasn't in the kitchen, she headed up the hall, her feet making no sound on the carpeted floor. She passed Amy's bedroom and looked inside. The child's bedroom furniture was there, but the mattress was bare and the room had been stripped of all her belongings. Wes was not there.

She passed the bathroom and saw in a glance that he wasn't there.

That left only one place, she told herself. He was in his bedroom—the bedroom with the empty closet, the furniture they intended to sell. The bedroom with all his memories.

Swallowing back the emotion rising to her throat, she stepped into the doorway.

Wes sat with his back to her on the edge of the bed, his elbows braced on his knees, and his head hung low. He was holding the picture of his dead wife.

Patrice, Laney thought, backing away quickly from the door. He had come here to mourn over Patrice. Did Wes come here every day to cry over her? her mind railed. When she had believed she was making progress, making him love her, was he really having a quiet little grieving affair with the ghost of his first wife?

An anesthetic numbness washed over her, blurring the lines of her life until the edges seemed unclear. It was turning out just like it had before. There was a baby, and its father didn't love her, and once again, she was left wondering what she was going to do.

She got into her car, nursing that numbness and backed out of the driveway without Wes even knowing she'd been there. She was halfway down the block before the numbness burst like a dam, and the tears assaulted her.

It was too good to be true, wasn't it, Lord? She should have known that God's provisions didn't go as far as she thought they had. Things weren't supposed to be so easy for her. There had to be a catch.

And now she knew there was. Patrice was still a player in this hopeless triangle of her marriage. Wes was never going to let her go. The house was like a shrine to her, where he went to pay homage when Laney didn't know it. She should have known—should have expected it. His love for Patrice had been too strong to put behind him.

She cried all the way to his office to pick up Amy, who was "helping" Sherry with her paperwork. Pulling herself together, she took Amy home and told herself that if Wes wasn't wholly hers, he wouldn't be completely happy about the baby. He would wish it were Patrice's instead of hers. Laney would see it in his eyes and hear it in his voice. It would destroy her ecstasy over her baby, and she wouldn't let him do that. This baby was going to be wanted.

She and Amy kept busy cleaning house when they got home, and she tried desperately to wipe the scene from her mind. Wes, bent over the picture of Patrice, clinging incessantly to what he could never have again.

Laney was distant when Wes got home, and when he asked her about her doctor's appointment, she was vague. "It was just a twenty-four-hour thing," she hedged. "I'm fine now."

But the way she averted her eyes when she said it and the distant way she stared off into space as they ate, told him she was not fine at all. He didn't press her, because he was afraid. Was she hiding something, the way Patrice had tried to hide her illness at first? Was she trying to protect him?

He went with her to tuck Amy in that night, and after the story and the song that Laney sang to her each night, Amy reached up and hugged Laney's neck. "I love you, Mama," she whispered shyly.

Laney caught her breath. "I love you too, sweetheart." A sudden rush of dizziness swept over her, coupled with abrupt nausea. She wanted to cry, to drag Amy out of bed and spin her around in a breathtaking hug, but she felt too weak. Instead, she tucked Amy in then felt her way from the bedroom as Wes followed. He caught her in the hall, slid his strong, gentle arms around her waist, and pressed his forehead against hers.

The depth in his luminous green eyes told her that what he was about to say had no ghosts blurring it. "I love you, too," he whispered.

Waves of emotion poured over Laney, and she closed her eyes, willing the room to stop spinning. Had they both said what she thought they had said? Desperately, she wanted to tell him how she had waited to hear that, how she'd wanted to say it, but all that escaped her lips was a murmured, "Wes . . . I'm going to be sick."

Alarm flashed in Wes's eyes again. He released her, and she made a mad dash for the bathroom. He waited until she could speak, then dropped down beside her where she sat on the bed with her head between her knees. "Laney, please, tell me what's wrong."

She wiped her eyes and looked up at him. Her complexion was pale, and she was breathing like a runner at the end of a marathon. "Just the excitement," she said. "She called me Mama." *And you said you loved me.*

"Laney, you wouldn't have gotten sick over that." He grabbed her shoulders, his hands trembling. His jade eyes grew misty, cutting through her heart. "Laney, I've got to know. Something's wrong with you, isn't there? What did the doctor say?"

She lowered her eyes. Could she tell him yet? *Should* she? "Nothing. I told you—"

"Tell me the truth!" he cried, shaking her. "I love you, Laney. Don't do this to me!"

She met his eyes, saw the paralyzing fear, saw the love that couldn't be denied, saw the anguish over the vague possibility of loving and losing again. He thought she was sick, like Patrice, and he was terrified.

Suddenly it didn't matter if his reaction hurt her. His feelings were more important. She had to tell him the truth.

Quickly her hands came up to frame his face. "I love you too," she said without thought. A tearful smile crept across her face, and she knew the time was right. He would be happy. "Don't be afraid," she said on a nervous breath. "I'm not sick. I'm pregnant."

A moment of stunned silence gripped them as he stared at her, and then a smile overtook his features like dawn peeking over the horizon. "You're pregnant? With a baby?"

The look on his face erased all the problems that had clouded her mind. His joy was irrefutable. Somehow she would put her disappointments away where she wouldn't think about them. "Isn't that the usual way?"

He laughed, the loud, rolling sound of a man waking up from a long sleep, and a tear rolled down his cheek. She kissed it away.

"A baby," he whispered. "A *baby*."

He lifted her up, as if she were suddenly fragile, and put her in his lap. She was smiling, beaming, but something amiss stole from her glory. His smile faded a degree. "Why didn't you tell me? Why did you seem so sad and distant when I got home? Aren't you happy?"

"Of course I am!" she said. "I was so excited when I found out that I've already started buying things." She swallowed, and the lines of worry that he'd seen so many times before creased between her delicate brows. Studying his face, she realized it was a time for honesty. No longer was there room in their lives for hedging. "Then I remembered the baby clothes at your house, and I went to get them. I found you there."

He waited for her to go on, and when she didn't, he prodded her. "Why didn't you come in? You could have told me then."

She looked down at the pattern on her skirt, traced it with her finger as a deep sigh escaped her. "I did go in. I found you in the bedroom, staring at Patrice's picture."

"And you thought . . ." His voice trailed off, and he started to speak and stopped. There was a poignant lift to his brows when the words finally came out. "Laney, I was saying good-bye. I packed that picture, along with everything else, in boxes and cleaned out the house. There's a 'For Sale' sign in the yard by now. I had expected it to hurt, and I'll admit that there were a few pangs of sadness when I was boxing everything up, but the relief and anticipation were better than the pain."

"You . . . you're selling the house?"

"Yes." He stroked her face with a rough knuckle. "I have a home here with you. And a future. I love you, Laney. When are you going to believe that?"

She stared at him for a fragile moment, desperate to believe.

"You said once that deep love was only for the lucky ones. Well, it's not luck, Laney. It's God's direct blessing. We've got it, and I won't let you think we don't."

When she only stared at him with bewilderment and amazement misting her eyes, he smiled. "Why can't you believe?"

She laughed and slid her arms around his neck. "Oh, I believe. I believe."

He kissed her then, a kiss that healed her spirit and branded her soul, a kiss that marauded and plundered, then returned her gifts a hundredfold.

He slid his hand across her flat stomach. "A baby," he whispered reverently against her lips. "Our baby."

In amazement, she set her hand on Wes's over the baby God had given them together, the one they would love and parent and nurture together. The one who would give her a second chance to do things right. As he kissed her again, Laney sent up a silent prayer of thanks. God's provision. It was so forgiving, so promising, so rich with blessings. It was, indeed, too good to be true. But God had made it true. He had given her a cloak of her own that finally fit.

And she had no intention of ever taking it off.

Dear Reader,

If you were moved by the story of Wes and Laney in *Never Again Good-bye,* you might enjoy reading an excerpt from Book 2 of my Second Chances series—*When Dreams Cross.* In it, I tell the story of Andi Sherman and Justin Pierce, two of Wes Grayson's friends from college whose long romance was destroyed by pride. Now, eight years later, they are forced to put aside that pride and the bitterness resulting from it, and work together to save the dreams they've each strived for years to build. As the title suggests, those dreams can merge . . . or collide unmercifully. I hope the story of Andi and Justin, and their struggle with the faith that binds them in a common goal, will touch your heart.

Terri Blackstock

When Dreams Cross
Chapter 1

The past was a funny thing. It had a way of catching up with you—no matter how fast you ran. Andi Sherman realized now that it was gaining on her.

There was no way around it. The Khaki Kangaroo cartoon was the only one that had the kind of characters she had wanted for her amusement park. But she had resisted choosing it, because she wasn't sure she was up to dealing with the baggage that came with it.

But letting personal feelings influence her business decisions would have disappointed her father, who had trusted her to take over his dream when others saw her as not much more than a kid. She had something to prove now. Even if it meant working with Justin Pierce.

Andi sighed. "It's perfect, Wes. That cartoon is the only one that strikes the right chord."

The builder nodded. "You chose it, Andi. You knew those characters were perfect for Promised Land the first time you saw them. I did, too."

Andi turned around in her leather swivel chair and stared down at some papers on her desk. Of course she had known it was perfect. But that was before she had learned that Justin Pierce was its animator.

Justin Pierce. She had counted on spending the rest of her life without seeing him again.

She raised her eyes to her old friend and the builder who would incorporate these characters into the rides. As he watched, he rolled a purple Tootsie Pop around in his mouth, one that he'd no doubt bought for his daughters. "It doesn't matter, though," she said, "Justin probably won't come anyway. He's already an hour and a half late."

Wes took the sucker from his mouth and surveyed the uncharacteristic tension on Andi's face. "Justin's not stupid. If he has any business sense at all, he'll come."

"If it were just business," Andi said in a hollow voice, "it wouldn't be that hard."

Standing up, she went to the window, hands jammed in the pockets of her slacks. The cool pink blouse she wore provided a soft contrast to the tan on Andi's arms. Absently, her hand went up to tuck a stray strand of hair into the French braid at the nape of her neck. If only she could put this off until another day, she thought.

"Andi," Wes said, his gentle voice cutting into her thoughts to remind her he was still there. "Eight years is a long time, and you were both practically kids. Don't you think he's put all that behind him by now?"

Andi breathed a silent laugh. She had never been able to completely put it behind her. But she had lost more when the relationship ended than he had. She turned back to Wes, who'd been friends with them both when they were all involved in a Christian discipling group in college. "Of course he has. I'm just worried about those resentments he had toward me the last time I saw him. They might get in the way of my offer."

Wes stood up and stuck the Tootsie Pop back in his mouth. "Those resentments were unfounded. And your father was wrong. Everything that happened was wrong." His words were slurred around the candy, making what he said seem less important, but Andi knew better. "Surely the past won't cloud a business deal like this."

Surely, Andi thought with a sarcastic lift of her brows. But unless Justin Pierce had changed, she knew there would be trouble.

When Dreams Cross

Available at Christian bookstores.

(ISBN #: 0-310-20709-6)

ZondervanPublishingHouse
Grand Rapids, Michigan
http://www.zondervan.com

A Division of HarperCollins*Publishers*

Also look to Terri Blackstock's Sun Coast
Chronicles for compelling romantic suspense.

Available now at a Christian bookstore near you!

Book #1
Evidence of Mercy
Terri Blackstock
Softcover 0-310-20015-6

Book #2
Justifiable Means
Terri Blackstock
Softcover 0-310-20016-4

Book #3
Ulterior Motives
Terri Blackstock
Softcover 0-310-20017-2

Coming April 1997!
Book #4
Presumption of Guilt
Terri Blackstock
Softcover 0-310-
20018-0

ZondervanPublishingHouse
Grand Rapids, Michigan
http://www.zondervan.com

A Division of HarperCollinsPublishers

About the Author

Terri Blackstock is an award-winning novelist who has written for several major publishers including HarperCollins, Dell, Harlequin, and Silhouette. Her books have sold over 3.5 million copies worldwide over the last twelve years, under two pseudonyms.

With her success in secular publishing at its peak, Blackstock had what she calls "a spiritual awakening." A Christian since the age of fourteen, she realized she had not been using her gift as God intended. It was at that point that she recommitted her life to Christ, gave up her secular career, and made the decision to write only books that would point her readers to him.

"I wanted to be able to tell the truth in my stories," she said, "and not just be politically correct. It doesn't matter how many readers I have if I can't tell them what I know about the roots of their problems and the solutions that have literally saved my own life."

Her books are about flawed Christians in crisis and God's provisions for their mistakes and wrong choices. She claims to be extremely qualified to write such books, since she's had years of personal experience.

A native of nowhere, since she was raised in the Air Force, Blackstock makes Clinton, Mississippi, her home. She and her husband are the parents of three children—a blended family which she considers one more of God's provisions.

We want to hear from you. Please send your comments about this book to us in care of the address below. Thank you.

ZondervanPublishingHouse
Grand Rapids, Michigan 49530
http://www.zondervan.com